BOUND BY MAGIC

A NEW ADULT FANTASY NOVEL

JASMINE WALT

DYNAMO PRESS

Cover illustration by Judah Dobin

Cover typography by Rebecca Frank

Edited by Mary Burnett

Electronic edition, 2016. If you want to be notified when Jasmine's next novel is released and get access to exclusive contests, giveaways, and freebies, sign up for her mailing list here. Your email address will never be shared and you can unsubscribe at any time.

AUTHOR'S NOTE

Dear Reader,

If this is the first book you've picked up in the Baine Chronicles series, I've included a glossary in the back of the book to help illuminate the backstory. If you've already read the first book, this glossary will help reacquaint you to the people, places and things introduced to you in the first book, Burned by Magic.

You can either read the glossary first to familiarize or re-familiarize yourself with Sunaya's world, or you can plunge into the story and refer to it as needed. The guide is in alphabetical order, and characters are listed last name first.

To the new reader, welcome to the Baine Chronicles! And to those of you who have read the first book, welcome back and thank you! Your support allows me to continue doing what I love most – writing.

Best, Jasmine

1
---

*S*ummer is my favorite time of the year, especially in Solantha. I love taking my steambike out on evenings like this, racing up and down the streets and soaking in the sights and sounds of my city. The briny air turns warm and inviting, the fragrance of ripening fruit and blossoming flowers softens the stench that clogs some of the streets, and the city itself goes into full swing, livened up by merchants, artists and performers plying their wares.

But instead of racing through the streets on my steambike or chasing after bounties, I was in Solantha Palace getting my ass kicked. And if you were standing here with me, you wouldn't even be able to tell it was summer.

"Sunaya!" Fenris called as I tucked and rolled across the wooden floor to avoid another frigid blast of magical energy. "You need to stop running away from the blasts!"

The ball of magic slammed into the wall behind me – or it would have, if the magical force field Iannis, the Chief Mage, had set up to protect the room hadn't flared to life. Instead, it bounced right off the wall just as I sprang out of my crouch, and

I twisted my body away hastily, putting Iannis right in the path of the evil, frigid missile.

The Chief Mage let out an annoyed sigh, then held up his hand. "*Gya'llerantha!*" he commanded, using one of the many Loranian Words I had yet to learn. Loranian was the magical language used in spellcasting, and the Words were incredibly difficult to memorize and pronounce. The ball of energy instantly changed shape, turning into a long tube of icy blue-white energy that Iannis sucked back up into his hand.

In seconds, it was as if the thing had never existed.

Frustrated, I bared my teeth at Fenris, who had opened his mouth to speak again. "Will you stop getting on my case about this?" I snapped. "I'd like to see *you* try to defend yourself against a ball of magic ice without freezing to death! Why don't you get down here and try it?"

"Because *you* are the one wearing protective armor. I'm just the referee." Fenris's lips twitched briefly before he regained control of his stern countenance. "You've got to stop being afraid of spellcasting, Sunaya, and use it to your advantage. Otherwise you'll never learn to properly defend yourself in a mages' duel."

"Gee," I said sarcastically, slanting my gaze toward the Chief Mage. "If I didn't know better, I'd say Fenris was my teacher, not you."

The Chief Mage gave me a look that was drier than desert sand. "Perhaps if you focused on the lesson instead of allowing yourself to be distracted by petty matters, you would be able to defeat me."

I rolled my eyes, then shot out my hand and blasted him with a fireball. The blue-green sphere screamed across the room, heating up the frigid air by several degrees as it barreled straight toward the Chief Mage. But unlike me, he didn't duck and roll out of the way, or even blink a single one of his long, dark lashes. He simply raised his hand again and blasted it with another stream of ice.

"That is *so* not fair." I glared at Iannis as a fine mist rained down from where the fireball had been, sprinkling the wooden floorboards. "If you'd just allow me to use my magic directly, instead of having to remember all these stupid incantations, this duel would already be over."

"You already know why you can't do that." Iannis folded his arms across his broad chest, tucking his long-fingered hands into his voluminous sleeves. He looked every inch the mage, dressed in a set of flowing blue and gold robes, his dark cherry wood hair pulled back from his handsome face into a low tail. I, on the other hand, looked more like a scrapper underneath the magical armor I wore, dressed in a pair of leather pants, lace-up boots, and a short-sleeved striped shirt, my mass of curly black hair flying all about as I moved. The Chief Mage had tried to get me into a set of robes once, but he'd failed miserably, so instead he kept giving me disapproving looks whenever I showed up for my training sessions – a vain attempt to shame me into wearing apprentice robes.

Just because I was half-mage didn't mean that I was going to start dressing like one, even if I was Iannis's apprentice. One could argue that since he was the Chief Mage and the governor of Canalo I had to make him look good in exchange for the honor of being his apprentice. But I didn't ask for any of this, and if I'd had my way I would still be out on the streets hunting down bounties and masquerading as a full-blooded shifter with no one the wiser. Not to mention those ugly dun-colored apprentice robes were *so* not my style. No way was I putting them on.

Getting out of spellcasting would be harder though, and I knew it. There were two ways to use the magical energy inside of me – one was by directing it with my thoughts, and the other was to use Loranian, the ancient language of magic used in spellcasting. I preferred the first method as it was faster and more intuitive, but I could last much longer in a duel using incantations than just blasting out energy with my mind. Like it or not, I had to learn how to do this if I was going to master my magic.

"Again," Iannis commanded, then immediately blasted me with another ball of ice magic.

This time I stood my ground, ignoring my shifter instincts, which were screaming at me to get the fuck out of there. As a species, jaguar shifters are fierce warriors, but we don't do magical duels. But as I was continuously reminded, I was also half mage, and I needed to start acting like one.

Mimicking the Chief Mage, I held up my hand and spoke the Loranian incantation he'd taught me, focusing my attention on the icy ball of energy hurtling toward me. The crystalline ball evaporated into a puff of steam, but I didn't have time to celebrate – as soon as it was gone Iannis hurtled another one at me.

"You know," I shouted at him after I'd dissipated the second missile, "if you lightened my workload at the Mages Guild I would have more time to practice my Loranian!" Feeling spiteful, I hurled another fireball in his direction.

"A likely story." Iannis gave me a skeptical look as he snatched the fireball right out of the air, breaking his rule of using only elemental-type spells – we'd agreed to that for the duration of the duel since Iannis knew far more spells than me, in an attempt to keep things fair. The fiery ball floated just above his palm before he spoke a Word that snuffed it out.

Show off.

"You and I both know that if I went looking for you, I would find you at the Enforcer's Guild begging Captain Galling for a docket."

"I don't beg," I snapped, affronted at the insinuation. "And so what if I do go to the Enforcer's Guild? I need to use my enforcer's license too. How am I supposed to afford my rent like this?"

The Chief Mage blasted me with another ball of icy energy. Incensed, I thrust my hand out and shot out another fireball. The two blasts collided in mid-air, then exploded, shaking the walls. Ice crystals rained down everywhere, clattering against the floorboards, and I stuck my tongue out at the Chief Mage as he scowled at me.

"It is no concern of mine if you can't afford that apartment," he said sternly. "You have a perfectly good room at the Palace available that you refuse to use, and access to the kitchens for food. You are more than welcome to move back in, but I am not reducing your hours at the Mages Guild. Every apprentice is required to put in time in order to earn their training."

"I'm not moving back in." This wasn't the first time Iannis had broached the subject, but I was determined not to budge. As much as I refused to admit it out loud, I was attracted to the Chief Mage, and the more time I spent with him the more these feelings seemed to grow. Since romantic and carnal relationships between masters and apprentices were taboo, I knew nothing could come of it. Besides, I hated the sense of isolation that came from living in the Palace, cut off from the rest of the city. Living outside on my own was the best thing for both of us, even if he didn't see it that way. "Just because I'm your apprentice doesn't mean I have to be dependent on you."

Iannis opened his mouth to answer, but he paused at a knock on the door.

"Who is it?" he called. I pressed my lips together, already knowing the answer. I'd recognize that delicate knock and flowery jasmine scent anywhere – I'd heard and smelled them enough times over the last month to make me sick.

"It's Director Chen, sir. May I come in?"

Fenris opened the door, and I didn't bother to hide my scowl as Lalia Chen, the Director of the Mage's Guild and Iannis's right-hand woman, stepped into the training room. Her red silk robes flowed around her tall, lithe form as she moved, a stark contrast to her ivory skin. She'd left her long, fine black hair unbound today, allowing it to flow around her oval face, and it swung forward in a dark curtain as she bowed. Her perfect, polished look only served to remind me how unrefined I was, and the sparks of jealousy she always incited in my chest burst into flame before I could stomp them out.

"I'm sorry to interrupt you, Lord Iannis, but urgent news has come up regarding the Convention. I'm putting together an emergency Council meeting to go over the revised agenda they sent in, and we need you to be there."

"Of course." The Chief Mage inclined his head to her, then turned back to me. "I'm afraid we will have to end our lesson early tonight, Miss Baine."

What else is new? I thought, anger bubbling up inside me. I was getting really tired of Director Chen cutting my lessons short, and I opened my mouth to tell Iannis as much. Yes, the lessons were frustrating, but dammit I needed him! And the part of me that wanted him couldn't help but hurt every time he left me hanging like this.

But then I glanced sideways at Director Chen, and the sight of her face, so calm, so serene, stopped me in my tracks. If I started whining right now, I would only look like a childish fool in comparison to her, which was the last thing I wanted. I didn't need another reason to feel inferior around her.

"Sure," I said with a shrug, as if I didn't care one way or the other. "I get that you've got a government to run. Go do your thing."

"We'll resume this lesson tomorrow night."

The two mages swept out of the room, leaving me alone with

Fenris. As soon as the door closed behind them, I let the mask slip from my face, allowing the anger in my heart to shoot back up to the surface.

"Sunaya," Fenris said, noticing the murderous look on my face. "You shouldn't be so angry with Iannis. He's never had an apprentice for as long as I've known him, and it's a big adjustment for him to find time to train you while also running the state."

"I get that, Fenris, but at the very least he could actually try to stick around for the whole hour he's penciled me in for," I snapped. "We only have lessons three times a week, and Director Chen has already taken him off to do other things several times in the past fortnight. And he wonders why I'm not making enough progress!" I threw up my hands.

"It won't be like this forever, you know." Fenris sighed, running a hand across his short, dark beard as he cut his yellow gaze away from me. He was a wolf-shifter, and though he couldn't have looked more different from Iannis with his shorter, stockier build and his dark tunics, the two of them were fast friends. Because of that, Fenris's commands had weight, which had been a huge help to me when I'd first arrived at the Palace as he'd used his influence to ensure I got enough food and to soften Iannis up towards me. "Iannis wants to keep a close eye on Director Chen after the fiasco with Argon Chartis. Once he's certain he can trust her, he'll be able to take more time away from the Mages Guild and focus on your training."

"I guess that makes sense," I muttered. Argon Chartis was the former Director of the Mage's Guild, and he'd been doing a crappy job, shuffling off matters that he felt didn't merit his attention, and hiding problems from the Chief Mage to make him think everything was under control. Truth be told, I was happy Iannis was rolling up his sleeves and digging into the corruption. With any luck things would start to improve for shifters and humans around the city.

But still, after losing Roanas, my mentor, to the silver murders a few months ago, I was feeling a little bereft. And though Iannis certainly wasn't a father figure to me as Roanas had been, I was still his charge, and it was frustrating that I couldn't rely on him.

"I still don't see why he can't keep his appointments with me or see them through all the way," I groused. "Can't he just tell Chen to wait another half-hour? I mean, she should know better than to butt in on my lessons when they're so infrequent to begin with."

"Things will get easier once the Convention is over," Fenris said. "You know how important it is that Iannis arrives at the capital properly prepared. Much as you might wish otherwise, this takes precedence over your lessons."

"Yeah, but I don't have to like it." I sighed, dragging a hand through my hair. The Convention was a biennial event held in Dara, the capital of the Northia Federation, where delegations from all fifty states gathered to debate and vote on legislation. I knew how important it was for Iannis and his delegates to be there and represent Canalo, and something like a last-minute agenda change was important enough for Director Chen to call an emergency council meeting.

"Well, I would stand here and talk to you, but regrettably I have other matters to attend to this evening." Fenris eyed me. "Will you be alright on your own?"

I flashed Fenris a grin, shaking off my melancholy mood. "I've been on my own a long time, Fenris. I think I can manage one more night."

I hopped on my steambike and rode down to the Port, the stretch of coastline a few miles east of Solantha Palace where seafaring merchants did business side by side with trendy boutiques and magical shops, the latter operated by foreign magic-users who'd obtained a special license to practice magic in the Northia Federation. Aside from rare cases like myself, they were the only people outside of the mage families allowed to practice magic in the Federation – everyone else born with magical powers either had to subject themselves to a magic wipe, or face execution.

I shook my head as I parked my bike outside Witches' End, the pier where the aforementioned magic shops stood, marveling at how my life had changed so drastically in two short months. As a shifter-mage hybrid, I'd lived under the threat of execution daily, hiding my forbidden magic and pretending that I was half-human rather than half-mage to those who could tell I wasn't a full-blooded shifter. But when my secret was outed, instead of executing me, the Chief Mage chose to take me on as his own apprentice so I could master my powers and prevent myself from accidentally hurting someone – which, according to the mages, was the whole reason why magic was forbidden to non-mages in the first place.

I'd always hated mages for their high-handed superiority and the status that had been afforded them through birth and circumstance, but the Chief Mage's offer to train me had started to chip away at some of my anger, and the more time I spent working at the Mages Guild, the more I got used to the stuffy bastards. No, I might not ever master their icy composure, or don their flowing robes, but I was beginning to embrace my magical side, and that was something I never thought would happen.

Looping my thumbs into my jean pockets, I walked down the pier, a bounce in my step as I headed over to Comenius Genhard's shop, *Over the Hedge*. Comenius was a hedge-witch from Pernia, a foreign country across the eastern sea. He specialized in nature magic, his shop part apothecary, part charm-shop. He was also one of my best friends, and between my apprenticeship and the few enforcer gigs I managed to get, I hadn't seen him in ages. I was looking forward to dragging him out of his shop for a stiff drink so we could catch up.

Unfortunately, Comenius was nowhere to be found, either in his shop or in the apartment above the building. Annoyed, I leaned against the glass storefront and stared out at Solantha Bay, my eye drawn to the Firegate Bridge, its glorious red towers glowing in the light of the dying sun. It was seven o'clock, and the shop should have still been open. Where the hell was Com? At the very least Noria, his assistant, should be here, but the CLOSED sign told me the shop was completely empty. The same thing had happened last time I'd dropped by two weeks ago, which was highly unusual.

Maybe he's out with his new girlfriend.

I pouted at the thought – not because I didn't want Com to have a love life, but because it reminded me that my own relationships were sorely lacking right now. Sure, I wasn't the only one in the single department – my friend Annia, Noria's sister, was still unattached as far as I knew – but Noria had Elnos, and with Com's time being taken up by someone too, I was feeling decidedly left out.

Shaking my head, I turned around and walked back up the pier towards my bike. I was being ridiculous. I'd never had much time for a love life before, and with my schedule monopolized by the Palace I certainly didn't have time now. There was no point in pining over something I couldn't have.

I slung my leg over the seat of my bike, then just sat there for a moment as I considered my next move. Maybe I should go track down Annia and see if she needed help with any of her current jobs. She'd thrown me a few bones the last couple of weeks, giving me some small local jobs that I could fit in between the cracks of my busy schedule, and she might have something for me now.

But as I scanned the crowds of people walking up and down the neat sidewalks of the Port, tourists and locals alike, I realized that I didn't want to work tonight. For once, I wanted to be one of those carefree people, talking and laughing and enjoying the beautiful summer night with someone else.

So instead of heading down to Annia's apartment in Maintown, I took off for Rowanville, leaving a white-hot cloud of steam in my wake as my engine let out a shrill whistle. I was going to have to load up on some more coal soon – the charm that magically replenished the water in the bike did not, alas, extend to the coal itself. Just one more expense to burden my alarmingly empty money pouch with.

A kind of nostalgia washed over me as I walked into *The Twilight*, the interspecies nightclub that had kept me financially afloat back when Garius Talcon, the former Deputy Captain of the Enforcer's Guild, was refusing to give me work. The colorful strobe lights reflecting off the black lacquered surfaces were as annoying as ever, but familiar, and I waved to Cray, the big black guy behind the counter that I used to tend bar with. He didn't smile, but he gave me a friendly nod, and I relaxed a little, relieved that he wasn't going to try and kick me out. My last day working in the bar, I'd left him in the lurch when Roanas had called me for help, and in fact I'd nearly ripped Cray's face off when he tried to stop me.

A pang of sadness for my dead mentor hit me in the chest, but I shrugged it off, determined to keep my spirits up tonight. Claiming one of the barstools for myself, I leaned forward on the counter and waited until Cray finished with his customer.

"Hey Naya," he said in his deep, slightly gravelly voice. "Been awhile since I've seen you. How are things?"

"Hectic," I said with a sigh, swinging my legs back and forth beneath the counter a little. "The Chief Mage keeps me pretty busy up at the Palace."

"I can imagine." His dark eyes swept over me for a second, and I could tell he had questions, but he didn't press. "You want your usual tonight?"

I hesitated, on the verge of ordering a shot of *teca* and amaretto on ice, but I decided against it. *Teca* was one of the few alcoholic beverages that could get shifters buzzed, but after being shot up with drugs two months ago and nearly killed, I wasn't in any hurry to be intoxicated again.

"Nah, I think I'll just take a virgin sex on the beach. And a bacon cheeseburger." My magic lessons with the Chief Mage always left me hungry, as using magic drew on my energy stores.

"Coming right up." Cray's lips quirked at the girly drink, and possibly the irony as well. There *was* something silly about ordering a "virgin" sex on the beach, but since I couldn't get drunk I didn't see the point of paying extra for the alcohol.

He served my drink with a cute little tropical umbrella, and as I sipped at the sweet, fruity concoction, waiting for my burger, I scanned the crowd to see if there was anyone interesting to talk to. To my surprise, I picked out Inspector Boon Lakin, hunched over the table in one of the booths toward the back of the club and away from the strobe lights. A fedora was perched atop his blond head, partially concealing his face, but I recognized the brown leather coat he was wearing even if the table did conceal most of it – that was definitely him.

Curious as to what he was doing here, I grabbed my drink and burger, which Cray had just delivered, and crossed the room. As I drew closer, I saw that Lakin was engrossed in a case file, which must have been why he didn't hear me approach. Even more interesting. Why would he bring his work to a place like this?

"Hey Lakin," I greeted him, and his head shot up as I slid into the seat across from him. I grinned at the startled expression on his rawboned face. "Long time no see."

"No kidding." Lakin's reddish-yellow eyes gleamed in the darkness as he regarded me, a small smile playing on his lips. "I think the last time I saw you, you were a few seconds away from punching Chieftain Baine in the face."

I snorted. I'd met Lakin, the new Shiftertown Inspector and Roanas's replacement, over two months ago, when I'd stopped by the Shiftertown Cemetery to say goodbye to Roanas and make my peace with his death. As it turned out, he'd received an emergency response call from my aunt Mafiela, the Chieftain of the Jaguar Clan, and I'd decided to tag along. My aunt and I had nearly come to blows during our impromptu family reunion, but I'd gained some valuable intel regarding the case I was working so I didn't regret it.

"So, what brings you here to the Twilight, and with your work, no less?" I gestured at the file on the table in front of him, which he'd closed when I sat down. "Figured you'd prefer the quiet of your office."

Lakin rolled his eyes. "I would, if it were actually quiet over there," he said. "The residents of Shiftertown find excuses to knock on my door at any hour of the day. I figured Rowanville would be a good place to escape them."

"Well I don't know if you'll find peace and quiet, but I'm sure nobody from Shiftertown will think to look for you here." Shiftertown was the section of Solantha where the different shifter clans resided, while most of the shifters that lived in this part of town were clanless. Rowanville was the melting pot of the city, the only place where shifters, humans and mages lived side-by-side, so a Shiftertown resident in need of an Inspector wouldn't be coming here to find him.

"Are you going to tell me what this current case is about?" I asked before taking a big bite out of my burger. I'd been looking for company, and now that I'd found it I wasn't planning on going anywhere.

Lakin eyed me for a moment, a debate going on behind his yellow-red shifter eyes. "I've actually been doing some more digging into the silver murders," he said, tapping the file. "This is the file Roanas had started on the matter, the one you asked Mr. Genhard to hand over to me. I've added a bit to it since then."

"No kidding." My eyes widened as I glanced down at the file – it was a good deal thicker than it was when I'd sneaked it out of Roanas' house and given it to Comenius to hold onto. Roanas had only just begun to dig into the silver murders before he was killed, so the details in the file had been pretty sparse when I'd recovered it. "What have you dug up so far?"

Lakin pressed his lips together, then opened the file and pulled out a photograph. "I found out that your enforcer colleague, Sillara Tarenan, had a human live-in partner named

Narina who lives in Rowanville," he said, sliding the photograph across the table. "I went to speak to her earlier, to find out if she knew anything that would explain why Sillara was targeted."

I picked up the photo of Sillara's lover, my heart sinking a little as I studied the smiling, heart-shaped face of a young woman with flowing pale hair. I had a feeling she wasn't smiling like that anymore.

Like me, Sillara had been an enforcer, and she'd been one of the earliest silver poisoning victims. She and I hadn't been close, but we'd been friendly and she was damn good at her job. Her murder stood out because she was the only shifter from Rowanville to be targeted, so it made sense for Lakin to be digging into her case. An old anger filled me at the senseless loss – if I ever got my hands on Petros Yantz, the bastard who'd organized the murders, I'd make sure he suffered for a long, long time.

"Did you learn anything?" I asked, handing the photo back to him.

"Nothing concrete," Lakin admitted, nursing his drink – a cup of coffee, judging by the scent wafting from it. I winced as he brought the cup to his lips – the coffee here was terrible. "But she did tell me that Sillara was involved in an important investigation."

I sat up straight. "What kind of investigation?"

"That's the thing – her partner doesn't know. She says Sillara didn't talk much about her work at home. However, she also told me that Sillara had been incredibly stressed in the weeks before her death – she'd toss and turn in their bed at night and was always on edge."

"Sounds like she was dealing with something big, then. Something that Yantz didn't want her to uncover." I forced down the anger that threatened to rise in my throat at the mention of Yantz's name – stewing about it would do me no good right now.

"That's what I'm thinking," Lakin said darkly. "My next move is to try and figure out what she was working on... but I'm not sure how cooperative the Enforcer's Guild will be about turning her files over to me."

"How about we both head on over there tomorrow?" I offered, excited at the prospect of doing something useful on this case. "I can twist some arms for you and help get what you need."

Lakin's lips twitched. "I'm sure you could," he agreed, then paused. "Is this going to interfere with your apprenticeship at all? I wouldn't want to put you on the Chief Mage's bad side."

I rolled my eyes. "I'm *always* on his bad side, so there's nothing new there." I was *not* going to let this stupid apprenticeship get in the way of my chance to participate in this investigation, the Mages Guild be damned. Surely they could find someone else to shuffle paperwork around tomorrow morning. This was far more important.

Lakin only shook his head. "Well you're a grown woman, and I'm not going to pass up your assistance when I could really use it." He smiled, and the expression softened his rawboned features. "I really appreciate your help with this, Sunaya."

"No problem." I smiled back as pleasure filled me. It had been a long time since I'd basked in the glow of appreciation, and I'd forgotten what it felt like. "I've been cooped up in the Palace for way too long. I'll be glad to finally have some action again."

Lakin glanced down at the file. "Somehow I get the feeling we're going to experience more than our fair share of action before this case is over."

He didn't know how right he was.

3

The next morning, I pulled into the small parking lot outside the Enforcer's Guild building, the sun just cresting the rooftops of the buildings lining the street. I figured the earlier we got this done, the sooner I could get back to the Mages Guild. Sure, I was due for a scolding either way, but they'd be less pissed at me if I was simply late rather than absent the entire morning.

As I sat on my steambike waiting for Lakin to arrive, I allowed my gaze to roam over the tall, dingy grey building that represented Canalo's law enforcement system. It was rectangular, four stories high, with cracked windows and stains sunk deep into the concrete walls. The state of the building was a perfect allegory of our current justice system – old, flawed and neglected. One of the reasons I'd become an enforcer was to try and make a difference in the system, and uncovering Yantz's role in the silver murders was the first time I'd made a dent in my goal. It felt good to finally be back in the trenches again, even if just for a short time.

A large shadow passed over my head, and I glanced up to see one of the new tourist dirigibles passing overhead, puffing out white steam that trailed across the morning sky. Half-open glass windows lined both sides of the small cabin fitted to the underside of the large, bright red transport, and I snorted at the sight of cheery humans leaning out and gleefully waving their hands. I was amazed the tour company allowed such a thing – if a tourist hadn't tumbled out one of those windows yet, it was bound to happen eventually. But dirigibles were a relatively new addition to Solantha's tourism industry, and I had to admit that enjoying the sunrise from up there sounded pretty fun. If I ever had some spare coin again, I'd have to get myself a ticket, even if they were pretty pricey.

The high-pitched whistle of Lakin's steambike drew my attention away from the dirigible, and I turned my head to see him enter the parking lot. He wore a helmet with a visor that covered his face, and the wind blew his long leather coat out behind him, which I had to admit looked pretty badass. Maybe I should get myself one of those things.

With what money?

I sighed, shoving my hands into the achingly empty pockets of my own leather jacket. Right. I was really going to have to do something about my money situation soon. The reward I got for my part in uncovering the silver murder conspiracy was drying out in my bank account, and the small stipend I received from the Mages Guild as an apprentice wasn't enough to cover my living expenses. If I didn't convince the Chief Mage to let me take on work at the Guild soon, I really *was* going to have to move back into the Palace. Most people in my situation would have happily taken Iannis's offer of free room and board without a second thought, but I knew the moment I did that I would lose my connection to the outside world. If I cloistered myself away in the Palace long enough, it would be all too easy to turn into one of these lofty, ice-hearted mages and lose touch with myself. And I'd be damned if that was going to happen.

"Morning," Lakin said as he tugged off his helmet. His blond hair was slightly tousled, making him look positively boyish as he grinned at me, and I was surprised at the answering flutter in my stomach. "You ready to twist some arms?"

"You bet." I grinned back as I hopped off my bike.

We drew curious looks from the enforcer trainees manning the front desk as we walked in through the front door, which I guess was only to be expected – Lakin was new in town, and I was something of a conundrum. When I'd dragged the Chief Mage into the silver murders, I'd brought the scrutiny of his office down on the Enforcer's Guild, and Captain Galling hadn't forgiven me for making him look bad. But on the other hand, I had the Chief Mage on my side, so Captain Galling couldn't do anything overt to make my life miserable. As a result, the other enforcers weren't sure how to react around me. Some were exceedingly polite, while others glared daggers at me and whispered nasty things about me when they thought I wasn't within hearing distance. I didn't know where the foreman of Sillara's crew stood, or whether his attitude toward me would make this easier or harder.

Lakin and I crossed the lobby, our boots clopping against the scuffed tile, and headed toward the elevator on the other side. The rickety box spit us out on the fourth floor, where the smaller crews' desks were located – while there were a few enforcers like me who worked solo, the majority of us worked as crews, each headed up by a foreman who answered to the Guild Captain. I sent a silent prayer up to Magorah, the shifter god, that Sillara's crew would still be here.

It wasn't too hard to find them – they were a group of five shifters, clustered toward the far left end of the room as their foreman, Laro Vanit, read off the names on their docket for today. I pursed my lips as I caught sight of the long list – there were at least twenty names on there, more than enough for their crew, and I wished I could snag one of their bounties for myself.

But that wasn't what I was here for.

"Excuse me, Foreman Vanit," I said after he was done. "Can I talk to you and your crew for a moment?"

Vanit turned slowly to face me, and if I were a lesser woman I would have been intimidated by the glare he shot my way. A brawny black male with tawny lion shifter eyes, a shaved head and blocky features, he stood a head and a half taller than me, and was looking at me as though I was vermin spawn.

Guess he was a member of the "I Hate Sunaya" camp. Tension curled its stiff fingers around my shoulders, and I stood up straighter, meeting his fiery gaze with my own.

"What do you want, Baine?" he snapped, folding his arms over his chest. He wore standard black mercenary leathers that were only a few shades darker than his skin, making him look like a creature of the night. "As you can see, we're a little busy around here. Unlike you, some of us have to work for a living."

The other shifters in his crew snickered, and I clenched my teeth at the insult. But if I rose to the bait, this would degenerate very quickly into a fight, and I needed to stay focused on getting those files.

"This is Inspector Lakin from Shiftertown," I said, gesturing to Lakin, who was quietly assessing the group from my left. "He's investigating Sillara's death, and needs to study the cases she was working on before she died. We were hoping you guys would point us to her files."

One or two of the crew members shifted uncomfortably at the mention of Lakin's name, but the rest looked bored or hostile. Like me, these shifters were all clanless, and wouldn't consider Lakin an authority figure.

"Hmph. I don't know about that," Vanit said, turning his

tawny glare onto Lakin. "Last I checked, Sillara's death wasn't a homicide. Why would you need to dig into it more?"

"It turns out the coroner was mistaken," Lakin said evenly, his eyes gleaming with impatience. "Sillara died of silver poisoning, just like Petros Yantz's other victims. Since she was a member of Shiftertown's tiger clan, her murder falls under my jurisdiction."

"I guess that makes sense," Vanit admitted, his scowl lessening slightly. But it returned with a vengeance as his gaze switched back to me. "I'd like to help you, Inspector Lakin, but since you're attached to this sell-out over here I'm afraid you'll have to appeal to Captain Galling directly. And as I recall, he's out of town." He gave me a vicious grin, baring his fangs.

"You asshole." I took a step forward, my lip curling back into a snarl of my own. "What the fuck is wrong with you? Sillara was your crew mate. I'd think you'd want her murder solved just as much as we do."

"Yeah, well she's been dead for over three months," Vanit spat. "I think the mystery can wait a few more days if it means I don't have to lower myself to help a whore like you."

"*Excuse* me?"

"Give me a break," Vanit sneered. "We all know that you're responsible for the shitty management changes that have been going on down here. Not only did you defect over to the mages' camp, but you're sucking mage cock so you can get what you want. So excuse me if I don't help you."

"I don't know where you heard that from, but I'm not sleeping with the Chief Mage." A hot flush spilled across my cheeks at the accusation, and my thighs quivered with the effort of holding myself back from attacking Vanit. "In case you didn't know, master and apprentice relationships are supposed to be platonic."

"Oh yeah? Well you coulda fooled me. *Whore*."

Lakin made a grab for my arm as I launched myself forward, but he was too late – I'd already closed the distance between myself and Vanit, my fist hurtling through the air towards him. Vanit side-stepped the blow, a smug grin on his dark face, but I wasn't going to let him get away that easily – I pivoted on my left foot, then side-kicked him in the midsection with my right. Grunting from the force of the blow, he doubled over slightly but recovered quickly, drawing the sword at his side as he straightened. I jumped backwards to avoid the slash of the steel blade, which gleamed in the light filtering in through the dingy, cracked windows.

Gasps and murmurs broke out all across the room, reminding me that there were several different crews here, and I stiffened. Vanit's crew was closing in on me with murderous stares, and though Lakin and I could probably take them all on with the help of my magic, I wasn't going to be able to fight off an entire room of enforcers if they decided to take Vanit's side.

"Hang on," Vanit said, his thick lips curling into a grin as he held up his hand in the direction of his crew mates. "Let's play this out. I think Little Miss Sunaya here's let her new position as the Chief Mage's pet go to her head, and I for one would like to remind her where she stands. What say you and I have a little match, huh?"

My eyebrows shot up. "You want to what, have a duel or something?"

"No, I want to kick your entitled little ass." He bared his teeth at me, fangs sliding out from beneath his gum line. "If, for some reason, you should happen to win, my crew will more than happily get Sillara's files for you."

"Sunaya," Lakin said, his voice low and urgent. "You don't have to do this. We can come back when the Captain is here."

"No." I glared at Vanit, unstrapping my crescent knives from my right thigh. "If Vanit wants a fight, he's getting one. Just because he's got his panties in a twist over me doesn't mean he's getting away with this. We're *getting* those files."

Vanit's expression turned downright ugly, and he shifted into a fighting stance, holding his sword aloft. I curled my fingers around the handles of my knives and took up a stance of my own, holding one knife out towards him and the other close to my midsection so I could block any blow that got past my initial guard, much like a traditional empty-handed stance. The other enforcers gathered around us in a circle to watch, their eyes gleaming with the thrill of an impending fight, and I saw quite a few of them exchange coins out of the corner of my eye.

If most of them were betting on Vanit, that didn't bother me. It just meant they were going to lose their money.

"Well, what are you waiting for?" I demanded. "Weren't you going to teach me a lesson?"

Vanit let out a snarl of rage, then rushed forward, jabbing straight for my mid-section with his sword. Magic crackled at my fingertips, and I itched to simply blast him with a fireball, but I knew the Chief Mage would be pissed at me if I ended up killing Vanit, so instead I simply caught the blade using one of my knives, then side-stepped him. Off balance, he had no time to move out of the way as I slashed down the length of his forearm with the knife in my right hand. Blood gushed from the wound, splattering across the front of my leather jacket, and Vanit howled in agony. His fingers went limp, the sword clattering to the ground, and I wasted no time, swinging my fist back around to my ear and then smashing it into the side of his jaw, a vulnerable spot regardless of the size and strength of an opponent.

Vanit dropped like a stone.

The resulting silence in the room was deafening. All eyes were on me, and my skin prickled under the weight of the crowd's attention. Ignoring them all, I nudged Vanit in the side with the toe of my boot just to make sure he was down. He groaned slightly, but didn't budge otherwise.

"Anyone else feel like challenging me?" I lifted my head to meet the eyes of the rest of Vanit's crew.

One by one, the rest of the shifters lowered their eyes submissively, accepting their defeat. No, they didn't hate me any less, but damn if they weren't going to respect me, and that was all I really cared about at this point. Now that I was finally out from Garius Talcon's thumb, *nobody* at the Enforcer's Guild was going to push me around anymore, no matter who they were.

"Very well," a dark blonde woman stepped forward from the rest of the crew, her gaze hot but steady on mine. "Come this way. I'll take you to the files."

---

4

*V*anit's crewmate took us to where Sillara's files were stored – which turned out to be in the basement, on the same floor as the jail cells I'd been forced to spend the night in after the whole city found out I was half-mage. There were several boxes of files, so Lakin and I had to call a cab to help transport them to his house in Shiftertown, driving alongside the cab with our bikes. No way was I leaving my steambike at the Enforcer's Guild parking lot – Vanit's crewmates were liable to slash my tires for what I did to their foreman, or worse.

"You really did a number on that guy, Sunaya," Lakin commented as we lugged the banker's boxes into his living room, admiration in his voice. The one-bedroom house was sparsely furnished, with only a single armchair and a low wooden coffee table in the living room. Still, the space was open and airy, with a large window that let in plenty of sunlight, and a fireplace that would make the space very cozy in the winter. "He looked like he was twice your weight, but you didn't even break a sweat when you took him down."

"Eh." I set down my stack of boxes on the ground, then

shrugged. "I'm used to fighting opponents bigger and stronger than me. That's why I have these." I lovingly patted my crescent knives, which were strapped to my thigh once more.

Lakin glanced at them curiously. "I don't think I've ever seen anyone use weapons like those before," he admitted.

"They're Garian-style weapons," I explained, sitting down cross-legged on the hard wooden floor so that we could start going through the boxes. "Great for close quarter fighting, and also for deflecting larger weapons. They've saved my hide more times than I can count."

"I'll bet." Lakin joined me on the floor, then turned his gaze toward the sea of boxes between us and sighed. "Let's start with the most recent one," he said, grabbing a box that was a few feet away from him. "That's probably where we're going to strike gold."

The first couple of files were pretty dull – they were all bounties for small time thieves or racketeers, stuff I'd seen a thousand times before – but the fifth file I opened proved to be much more interesting.

"Get this," I told Lakin, scanning the first page. "Looks like Sillara was looking into some shifter disappearances."

Lakin raised his gaze from the file he was looking through. "Shifter disappearances? You mean kidnappings?"

"Not sure." I shrugged as I flipped through the notes in the file. "As far as I can see there were no ransom notes left, or any demands made on the family members of the victims. They just disappeared, and were never heard from again."

"Huh." Frowning, Lakin moved some of the boxes aside so he could sit next to me. "Is there anything tying the victims together other than the fact that they're shifters?"

I pursed my lips. "According to Sillara's notes, they're all in their early twenties, and nearly all of them are clanless, with the exception of one." I pulled out a letter and passed it to Lakin.

Lakin's eyes widened as he read the letter, which was the original request sent in to the Enforcer's Guild that sparked the case. The letter had been sent from a wolf shifter family that belonged to the Solantha wolf pack, several days after their son Tylin had gone missing.

"I remember that name, Tylin." Lakin looked up at the ceiling, tapping his chin in thought. "Roanas had a file on him too. From what I understand, he wasn't able to find out what happened to the boy, and the family just assumed he'd defected to the Resistance."

"I bet that's what a lot of the families ended up thinking." I pulled out the list of names, my heart sinking as I read through them again. Many young shifters, especially the ones born into poorer families, ran off to join the Resistance in hopes of a better future. The clans tried to take care of their own as best they could, but the government levied heavier taxes on the shifter community, and in return for leaving shifters alone they expected them to take care of the majority of their own welfare programs and civic upkeep. The Chief Mage, who wasn't from Solantha, had seemed surprised when I'd mentioned this to him, and with any luck he might dig into this issue eventually and help out Shiftertown and the other shifter communities scattered across the state. But from what I understood, the Chief Mages who ran the other forty-nine states in the Northia Federation were more than happy with the arrangement. As far as they were concerned, mages had created shifters, and if they weren't allowed to use us as slaves anymore, they weren't going to help us either.

Lakin and I spent the next half hour going through Roanas's missing persons files, cross-referencing them with Sillara's list. We crossed off every person who was a known member of the Resistance, and unsurprisingly, the majority of the names we were left with matched up with Sillara's list.

"I wonder how she compiled this list," Lakin murmured, staring down at the two sheets of paper, which he'd laid out side by side on the coffee table. "I see how she got Tylin's name, but her notes on the others are sparse. It's almost as if they've gone missing."

I frowned. "If someone went to the trouble of taking the notes, why wouldn't they just take the entire file? Seems like extra work to me."

Lakin shrugged. "I've worked on cases where I felt it necessary to keep the most important notes in a separate file at home, away from my office, where my deputies and others couldn't access them. It's possible Sillara did the same."

I nodded – that made sense. I couldn't count the number of times I'd taken work home with me. "So that means either the separate file is still at her home somewhere, or it's been destroyed."

"Sillara's partner said there were no work-related papers at their place. I'll have to question her again to see if there was any sign of a break-in recently." Lakin braced his hands on his knees, then pushed himself to his feet. "In the meantime, though, I'd like to go ahead and interview the families and friends of the shifters on this list. Perhaps something new will come to light."

"I'll come with you." I rose to my feet as well, eager to continue tugging on this thread.

Lakin hesitated. "I don't want you to take this the wrong way, but I think the interviews would go easier if you didn't come along. The residents of Shiftertown ... well, they're not sure how to feel about you just yet."

I opened my mouth to protest, then closed it again. Lakin was probably right. The shifter community wasn't friendly towards mages to begin with, and on top of that I was a reject of the Jaguar Clan. Nobody around here was going to be welcoming me with open arms.

"That's alright," I said casually, as if Lakin's rebuff didn't bother me. "I've got to get back to the Palace anyway."

A look of chagrin shadowed Lakin's eyes. "Sunaya –"

"No, seriously, it's fine." I held up a hand, not wanting his pity, and flashed him a grin. "You'll let me know if you dig up anything interesting, right?"

"Of course." Lakin's face relaxed into a smile, clearly deciding to let it go. "I really appreciate your help today," he said as he walked me out.

"Anytime." I looked over my shoulder as he held the door open for me and winked. "Just make sure you have something for us to sit on the next time I come over."

I turned away, then trotted down to the sidewalk where my steambike waited for me. As I looked around at the rows of houses lining the street, the realization struck me that I was out of touch with the shifter community. Ever since I'd moved out of Roanas's house and taken up residence in Rowanville to be closer to the Enforcer's Guild, I'd stopped coming to Shiftertown except on business, and as a result I didn't really know what was going on. When I was under Roanas's care, I'd often tagged along with him on errands, and aside from the Jaguar Clan the rest of the community had tolerated me just fine. There were a few grandmothers who gave me tea and cookies, and I'd had both shifter and human friends at school – one of the few civic programs Canalo *did* fund for everyone in the state. But I hadn't seen any of those people in a few years. By Magorah, for all I knew those grannies could have passed away by now.

So instead of heading down the hill and back towards Solantha Palace, I drove in the opposite direction, heading toward the Cat's Meow, a popular diner run by the Tiger Clan. It stood proudly near the center of Shiftertown, sandwiched between a welder's shop and a florist, the storefront wall painted a dark orange with black stripes running across diagonally. My lips twitched at the outrageous paint job – that was one thing that hadn't changed.

Rather than parking my bike in front of the diner, I went around the block, then ducked into an alley. Closing my eyes, I mumbled the Words to the illusion spell Iannis had taught me, envisioning myself as a tigress shifter with short blonde hair wearing a pair of jeans and a conservative sweater. If I went in there as myself no one would talk to me, but I also didn't want to look too attractive and draw attention I didn't want. I made sure to add an extra layer of illusion to mask my scent before I sauntered around the block and into the bar.

Like the exterior, the inside of the diner was much the same as it had been when I'd left Shiftertown – rows of orange and black booths along both walls, tables scattered in the open space between, and a bar dominating the center that stood bastion between the dining area and the kitchen. It was around ten in the morning, and though the place wasn't packed a good portion of the booths and tables were taken up.

I chose a seat at the bar, the best place for me to listen around and strike up a conversation if needed, and ordered a stack of pancakes since I hadn't had time for breakfast this morning. The food arrived quickly, and I tuned my sensitive ears into the buzz of conversation around me, hoping to hear something of interest.

"... we're going on vacation to Naraka next weekend," a woman was saying, her voice high pitched with excitement. "I can't wait!"

"Naraka?" the other woman asked, sounding amazed. "That's across the Western Sea, isn't it?"

"It's a nation of islands, right off the coast of Garai," the woman said. "We've never had the money to go abroad before, and my mate is so excited!"

"... I'm going to invest in the mining business," someone else, a male, was saying, his voice lower than the woman's. "Someone recently told me about a great opportunity in the mines up north."

"Mining?" another male scoffed. "I've never taken you for a businessman before. Listen, pay off your house and buy up as many supplies as you can. With the rebellion coming, you don't know how the economic landscape's going to change."

I gave my plate a bewildered frown as I continued listening to the conversations in the room. About half the people here seemed to be talking about finances -- investments or vacations or paying off debts – which I wasn't used to hearing from shifters. Most of us don't have a ton of money, and the conversations I remembered when Roanas used to bring me here usually revolved around the shifter community's discontent with the status quo. But today everybody seemed hopeful, optimistic even.

"Hey there." A male tiger shifter with dark, shaggy hair and orange eyes sat down on the bar stool next to mine. "Don't think I've seen you around here before."

"I'm not from around here." I smiled, dragging my attention from my thoughts and focusing them on the male next to me. "Just visiting from Parabas, actually," I said, pulling the first town that came to mind – the city up north that Lakin had transferred from.

"Oh really?" the male's eyes brightened. "It's beautiful up there – so much greener than Northern Canalo."

"True, but Solantha Bay is lovely too," I gushed, easily slipping into the role of tourist. I'd spoken to enough of them that I knew how to behave like one. "The Firegate Bridge is just *spectacular.* Have you ever walked across it?"

We chatted together for a little while as I finished my

pancakes, and though I tried to keep things friendly it was clear the guy was trying to hit on me. So after I was done, I reached into the money pouch tied to my belt to settle up so I could head out.

"Oh don't worry about that," the male said, pulling out a pandanum coin and several bronze ones from a large money pouch. "I've got it."

"No kidding." I stared down at the pouch, wondering how I hadn't noticed it before. "Say, I noticed a lot of people seem to be flush in these parts. Did the Canalo government give some kind of handout to the shifters here?"

"Oh, you mean this?" the male laughed, hefting his pouch. "No, this definitely isn't from the government. This is thanks to Sandin Federal Bank."

"Sandin Federal Bank?" I blinked. They were one of the largest human-owned banks in the Northia Federation. "They're handing out free money now?"

"Practically," the male said with a grin. "They've been advertising interest-free loans specifically for shifters, and a lot of us have cashed in on them."

"Seriously?" I sat up straight and looked around the room again. "That explains why everyone's talking about going on vacation." Maybe I could cash in on some of this "free" money too. I was certainly going to need it if the Chief Mage wouldn't let me get back to making a living soon.

"Yeah, no kidding. My parents are planning a trip to the East Coast." His eyes twinkled. "Maybe I'll go up and visit Parabas sometime, see if you're in town."

"Oh sure," I said with false enthusiasm. "You should definitely do that." I made a show of checking my watch. "Sorry, but I'm gonna be late for a meeting. I'd better go."

"Wait!" he grabbed my arm. "Are you sure I can't buy you a drink later?"

Later on, he wouldn't even recognize me. But rather than turn him down, I scribbled a fake phone number onto a napkin, then made a quick exit, heading for my bike in the back. I had one more stop, and then I needed to haul my ass to the Palace before the Mages Guild decided to do it for me.

5

This time Comenius's shop was open for business, the front door propped open to allow the cool sea breeze to waft inside. I stepped into the shaded, homey interior, inhaling the scent of herbs and candles, and smiled at the sight of customers inspecting the various charms and potions and making purchases. I remembered when Comenius had set up shop here several years ago as an unknown. I'd been one of his first customers, wandering into his store to see what he charged for protection charms because the guy I used to go to was charging me an arm and a leg. The two of us had connected quickly, and we'd even tried to make a go of a relationship, but that didn't last. Still, we were good friends, and I was glad to see how far he'd come.

"Naya!" Comenius smiled at me from behind the counter, his cornflower blue eyes lighting up. He was tall and lanky, dressed in a dark green tunic and brown trousers, his ash blond hair curling ever so slightly around the edges of his square jaw. "It's been too long," he said, coming around the counter to embrace me.

"Hey Naya!" Noria Melcott, his part-time assistant, paused in the middle of ringing up a sale to wave at me with a grin. She looked the same as ever, her wild red curls exploding around her small, freckled face, still wearing the same loud short-sleeved shirts and multi-pocketed pants that hid all kinds of tools. A techie to the bone, Noria loved to work with gears and gadgets, and I was surprised she worked for Comenius instead of a shop that could put her talents to use. But I wasn't about to object – at least this way I could see them both at the same time.

"Hey you," I called back as I embraced Com. His woodsy herbal scent engulfed me, and I took a moment to inhale deeply. Comenius's presence was always soothing to me; it was one of the reasons I was drawn to him even though these days we weren't more than friends.

"I dropped by yesterday to see if you wanted to hang out, but you weren't here," I scolded, drawing back so I could peer up into his square face. "What's up with that?"

"He was hanging out with Elania last night, of course," Noria called out in a teasing tone. "She showed up here in a tight black dress right about an hour before closing time and told him she needed some help with making dinner. I've never seen him close up shop so fast!"

"Zum Donnerwetter!" Comenius exclaimed as I chuckled, a pale pink flush splashing across his cheeks. "Do you have to say that so loudly in front of everybody?"

"What?" Noria shouted over the chiming of the cash register. "I can't hear you over the sound of all the money I'm making for you!"

I couldn't help it – I laughed. "She's one of a kind, isn't she?" I teased, giving Comenius a consoling pat on the shoulder.

"You could say that," Comenius said dryly, turning his gaze back toward me. "So what brings you here today, Naya? Did you drop by just to say hi?"

"I wish." I sighed, glancing out the window at the sparkling blue bay. Hanging out with Comenius at his shop sounded like paradise, but that wasn't in my future for today. "I actually came by to talk to you about the silver murders."

"The silver murders?" Comenius's pale eyebrows drew together in a puzzled frown. "What about them? Has someone else been poisoned?"

"No, no, nothing like that." I glanced at the doorway as the last customer exited the shop. "Is there any chance we could sit down for a moment and go over this?"

"Of course." Comenius waved Noria from behind the counter, and we settled into the wicker chairs grouped together to form a seating area a little ways off from the front desk.

"So what's going on?" Noria asked, concern in her dark eyes. "If it's something to do with the silver murders it's got to be serious."

I sat back in my chair and told them about how I'd run into Inspector Lakin, and how he'd just come from interviewing Sillara's lover. I filled them in on the details we'd found, telling them about the disappearances and how none of the victims' families had received any ransom notes.

"How strange," Comenius said. "So these shifters have all been disappearing?"

"All within the span of the last year or so," I confirmed. "I was thinking maybe we could pick through those old Shifter Courier papers you have and see if we can't dig up anything else useful."

"Of course." Comenius turned to Noria. "Would you mind getting them for me?"

"Sure thing." Noria hopped to her feet, then disappeared around the counter and into the back.

"So," Comenius said. "How is your training going at the Palace?"

I groaned. "I don't wanna talk about it."

"That good, eh?" Comenius's lips twitched. "The Chief Mage must be putting you through your paces."

I snorted. "Yeah, for a very small amount of time every week. The rest of the time I'm running around the Palace or the city doing grunt work for the Mages Guild in exchange for all the wonderful training I'm not getting." I sighed in disgust. "I probably get the least amount of training of all the apprentices at the Guild."

Comenius frowned. "Yes, but at least you're finally learning how to use your magic. And more importantly, you're alive. I think that's worth having to put up with a teacher who has limited time to train you."

I rolled my eyes. "Figures you would take the Chief Mage's side." But Comenius was right. If Iannis hadn't decided to claim responsibility for me and make me his apprentice, I would have been executed for the crime of having a magical talent without being born into a mage family.

Technically, I did have a mage family somewhere in the world, but I had no idea who my father was or any family he might have. So I'd been born into Solantha's Jaguar Clan, and since my late mother's older sister, Mafiela, was the Clan Chieftain, I'd been accepted into the clan without question, the secret of my birth kept from all but my immediate family. Unfortunately my aunt Mafiela couldn't stand me, because in her eyes I represented the bastard who'd knocked up my mother and ruined her chances of getting a proper mate; so when my mother had died I'd found myself on the streets not too long after that.

So much for family.

No matter how I looked at it, I owed the Chief Mage everything, and I knew I should probably be more understanding of his position. But shifters are emotional by nature, and I had feelings for him that I did my best to suppress, feelings that were constantly being hurt by his absence and neglect. It didn't help matters that once or twice I'd been convinced that he had feelings for me too. And it *definitely* didn't help that our Master/Apprentice relationship didn't allow for those feelings.

By Magorah, but I wished I could put my emotions aside the way Iannis did so effortlessly. My life would be much easier.

"Here we go," Noria called, coming back into the room with a stack of old papers in her arm. She dropped them onto the low wooden coffee table with a loud *thump*, then plopped back down into her chair. "So, where do we start?"

We divided up the papers amongst ourselves and aside from a few customers here and there, spent a mostly uninterrupted hour going through them, checking for any references to shifter disappearances. As I half-expected, we only found a handful – the article regarding Tylin, and two more concerning clanless shifters who just so happened to work in Shiftertown.

"Ugh." I tossed the last paper down onto the table in disgust. "I don't get it. There were at least twenty names on Sillara's list. There should be more than just three articles here!"

"Well, you did say most of them were clanless shifters," Noria pointed out. "The Shifter Courier mostly focuses on Shiftertown happenings, so maybe they just didn't feel like covering those other stories."

"Normally I would agree with you," Comenius said slowly, setting down his own paper, "except that the Shifter Courier has been struggling for a while now, and they need good content. Even though the majority of these victims weren't Shiftertown residents, their disappearances would still have been of interest to the Shifter Courier's readership. I have to agree with Naya – it is quite suspicious that there has been so little coverage."

"Just like the silver poisonings," I pointed out, crossing my arms over my chest. "Say what you want, Noria, but this whole thing stinks of a cover up. I want to go and investigate the

Courier and find out what's going on over there. Yantz was the one pulling the strings over at the Herald; I don't see why the same thing couldn't be happening over at the Courier too."

Noria opened her mouth to say something, but the telephone on the counter rang. Comenius sighed, then got up to go answer it.

"Over the Hedge. How can I help you?"

"Good afternoon," a cool female voice answered. My sensitive ears picked her up clearly, and I froze – that was Dira, one of the secretaries at the Mages Guild. *"Can you please inform Sunaya Baine that she is expected back at Solantha Palace immediately? The Chief Mage requires her presence."*

"Certainly." Comenius slanted me an arch look as he spoke. "I will send her over right away."

"I'm guessing you didn't have the morning off?" Noria asked with a grin as Comenius hung up the phone.

"No," I grumbled, shoving myself to my feet. Dammit, I'd been caught red-handed. "Guess I'd better head back to the Palace and find out what my Lord and Master wants."

"Try some humility," Comenius called as I strode out the door. "I find that works best when you're apologizing for something you've done wrong."

I bared my teeth at the idea. I had a few ideas about things I wanted to say to the Chief Mage when I saw him, but an apology definitely wasn't on the list.

6

By the time I skidded to a halt outside the manicured grounds of the Palace, I'd worked myself up into a fit of righteous indignation. The sun blazing high above my head seemed to champion my thoughts, and I marched up the walkway with my shoulders back and my head held high, determined not to look like I was crawling back to my master with my tail tucked between my legs.

I took the steps of the wide staircase two at a time, the white stone edifice of the Palace looming up above me, majestic as ever with its red-tiled roofs and proud turrets that speared the gorgeous blue sky. The large, elegant foyer I stepped into was equally impressive, the sun shining in through the tall, stained glass windows splashing colorful patterns onto the walls, the oil paintings, the parquet floor and the thick, expensive rugs that covered it. Canter, the old, grizzled mage who manned the reception desk, gave me a disapproving glare from behind his hooked nose.

"You're late."

"Thanks for pointing out the obvious." I rolled my eyes at the supercilious look on his wizened face – Canter hated me, and no doubt his shriveled little heart was bouncing up and down with glee at the idea that I was about to get a scolding from the Chief Mage. Ignoring him, I made my way up the right side of the double staircase that curved around both sides of the foyer, and down the carpeted hallway towards the West Wing, where the Chief Mage's study was.

It wasn't too long before I found myself in front of the familiar carved mahogany door, and I sighed, tracing the elegant patterns carved into the wood with my eyes. It seemed that every time I came to this room, it was always so that I could get into a fight with the Chief Mage. And even though it was in my nature to balk and fight, there was a part of me that wished that for once he would summon me to his study for a pleasant reason, like telling me that I was doing such a good job shuffling papers around, or that he was going to take off the restrictions he'd placed on my power level so I would have full access to my magic.

If wishes were steambikes, I thought, and pushed open the door.

The Chief Mage looked up from the report he was studying, his violet eyes narrowed in annoyance. "I see you've forgotten the art of knocking."

"Yeah, well you don't wear pants, so I figured there was no chance of catching you with them down or anything," I quipped, shutting the door behind me. "Would you like me to go back out into the hallway and try again?"

Something suspiciously like humor flickered in Iannis's eyes, but his stony expression didn't budge. "Sit down," he ordered, gesturing to one of the two chairs in front of his desk.

I did as he asked – if we were going to fight, I might as well make myself comfortable. Settling myself into the low, cloth-covered scoop chair, I crossed my right ankle over my left knee and clasped my hands in my lap, then looked at him expectantly, waiting for him to make the first move.

"Well?" he finally demanded. "Where have you been all morning?"

"I've been working on an investigation," I said evenly, determined to hold onto my temper for as long as possible. "You know, because that's what enforcers do."

His iridescent eyes turned glacial. "You're my apprentice first and foremost. I expect you to act like one."

"I *do* act like one, ninety-nine percent of the time," I snapped, digging my fingers into the arms of my chair. "Don't pretend like I haven't been working my ass off every day at the Mages Guild, because I have. But there was no way I was going to pass up the opportunity to work on this investigation, no matter *what* you say my schedule is."

"I see." The Chief Mage's icy expression didn't change one iota, and I sighed, wondering if he really *did* see. There were times when he showed glimpses of compassion, but for the most part he was like a rock wall – completely impenetrable without the assistance of explosive devices. Which probably explained why I blew up at him so often.

"What is this investigation that was so burningly urgent?"

"Oh, you don't know?" I asked mockingly. "I figured you'd know what I was doing, since you magically seemed to know exactly where to have your secretary call this morning."

Iannis gave me an impatient look. "I put a tracking spell on you after you were kidnapped by Yantz, so that I could find you again should you end up in a similar situation."

"You *what?*" I jumped to my feet, anger pumping hard through my veins.

"The last time we were incredibly lucky that someone had seen Yantz and Talcon carrying you into his house, or we never would have gotten to you in time," Iannis snapped. "Since you insist on gallivanting around the city and sticking your nose into trouble instead of staying at the Palace where it is safe, I put the tracking spell on you."

"You have no right." I forced the words out through gritted teeth, my hands trembling with the shock and anger of his betrayal of my privacy. "I'm not your property, *Lord* Iannis, to do whatever you like with. You can't just go putting spells on me like that, especially without even telling me!"

Iannis slowly rose to his full height, his violet eyes gleaming dangerously down at me. "Might makes right," he said softly. "I am the Chief Mage of this state, and I am also your master. Your life is my responsibility –"

"Bullshit!" I slapped my hand down on the desk, and a triangular paperweight jumped under the force of the blow. "You can't go throwing around the master-apprentice card, not when you've been such a crappy master to begin with!"

Iannis's expression froze. "Excuse me?"

A shock of fear rippled through my nerves as the energy in the room shifted, but it wasn't enough to make me back down – I was tired of this one-sided relationship, and damned if I was going to be silent about it any longer.

"You're probably the worst master in the entire Mages Guild!" I shouted. "You saddle me with all this grunt work because I'm supposed to be paying for my 'training', and yet we only have three lessons a week, lessons that you constantly cut short or cancel on! And then you have the nerve to tell me that I'm not improving enough!" My nails lengthened into claws that bit into the flesh of my palm, claws that I wanted to rake across his face. "You're a fucking hypocrite, and you know it!"

"That is *enough*." The Chief Mage's voice darkened, and magic began to crackle in the air around him, raw power sizzling in the shape of tiny blue sparks. If I'd been in beast form, the hair along my spine would have shot straight up – the Chief

Mage only got like this when he was truly furious. It took every-thing in me to stand my ground – my instincts were screaming at me to lower my eyes and back away before he smote me with a bolt of energy.

But I knew the Chief Mage wasn't going to kill me. After all, as he kept reminding me, I was his *apprentice.*

"I assure you Miss Baine, if you think I have been lacking as a teacher, you will change your mind after tonight. I will push you harder than you've ever been pushed in your life, until you *beg* me to let you out early." His tone was arctic, a direct contrast to the violet blaze in his eyes, and a chill of foreboding raced down my spine as he held my gaze in silence.

"Get out of my sight and report to the Mages Guild," he finally said. "If I find out that you've been anywhere else, I will close the seal your father placed on your magic. *Permanently.*"

I SPENT the rest of the afternoon stewing at the Mages Guild, which was a series of offices located in the South Wing of the Palace. Sitting in a cramped chair at a small table, I wasted the hours away prepping form letters from the Secretary of Agricul-tural Magic to go out to all the farms in the state. Stamp, stamp, stuff, lick.

Clerical work. Day in, day out, I was fucking doing clerical work. Yeah, sometimes they switched it up, sending me out into the city to pick up supplies, or pastries for a meeting or event, but mostly it was just mind-numbing paperwork. You'd think that as the Chief Mage's apprentice I'd be afforded some status, but Iannis must've told them to treat me like any other low-level apprentice. Worse, even. The other apprentices actually got to go out with maintenance crews every once in a while to reinforce the wards on the city or other magic-related tasks, but I'd yet to be chosen to do anything like that.

Probably because you suck at spellcasting.

I ground my teeth. I wouldn't suck at spellcasting if I had a teacher who spent more than three hours a week with me. Just because I wasn't raised in a mage family didn't mean I was stupid. In fact, for someone who'd been forced to suppress their magic for the last twenty-four years, I thought I was actually doing okay. I'd used my magic to conjure fireballs, breach wards, and create illusions. How many apprentices of my level could say *that*?

The hours dragged on, and yet by the time the pinkish-orange light of sunset began to filter in through the window on my left, I felt none of the usual relief or elation at finally being allowed to leave. Instead, a sense of foreboding filled me at the thought of my lesson with the Chief Mage tonight. I'm sure Magorah, the shifter god, was shaking His head at me from above for my foolishness – I'd wanted the Chief Mage to pay attention to me and I'd achieved that, but I'd also gotten more than I bargained for.

Gee, what else is new?

I thought about dawdling at the Mages Guild a little bit longer – a sure indication of just how much I was dreading tonight's lesson – but I knew that being late would only make things worse. So instead I carted myself down to the kitchen to grab some food so I would have something in my belly before my training started.

The scent of roasted lamb and freshly baked bread hit my nostrils long before I reached the staircase leading from the foyer down to the kitchen, and my stomach grumbled, redirecting my worries toward a more immediate need – nourishment. Shifters have a higher metabolism than humans and mages, and though that metabolism gives us stronger muscles and faster healing powers, it also means we have to eat a lot. I always kept food in one of the small pouches strapped across my body in case I needed an energy boost, and with the magic lessons on top of everything I was eating more than ever.

My monstrous appetite might have had something to do with why the head cook gave me a dirty look when I walked into the kitchen. I grinned at her, and she shook her head, then ordered one of her juniors to get me some food. A few minutes later, I was sitting at a small table in the corner, wolfing down a whole roasted chicken and a pile of herbed potatoes. I moaned quietly as the juicy flavors saturated my tongue – by Magorah, but the Palace had excellent food.

I could have gone to sit in the dining hall and eat, of course, but I didn't want to risk running into the Chief Mage yet, and I also wasn't totally comfortable sitting and talking with the other mages. They all had mixed feelings about me ranging from ambivalent to downright hateful, but there was one thing they all agreed on – I was not one of them. And no matter how good I got as a mage, I never would be. My shifter eyes and emotional attitude would always set me apart from them, even if I did put on a set of mage robes.

As I ate my food, my eyes wandered around the wide, open space of the kitchen, watching the chefs hard at work chopping, sautéing and stewing. The glint of a kitchen knife being raised in the air sent me flashing back to the time I'd snuck down here to grab some food in the middle of the night – my first night in the Palace, actually. A group of guards had found me down here, and had decided to make easy sport of me. I'd managed to defeat most of them, but I'd been starving and depleted of energy, unable to shift, so in the end they'd gotten the upper hand. If Fenris hadn't intervened, I might have died that night. He'd chased off the guards, then brought me straight to Iannis, who'd healed me.

A hazy image of Iannis's face looming above me, tight with concern, drifted into my mind, and guilt stabbed me in the chest. I'd never thanked Iannis for his help that night – I rarely thanked him at all, in fact, because I'd been so angry at the injustice of being held captive and threatened with execution for the simple crime of being born. I'd held him personally responsible for all that was wrong in our society, and sometimes I still thought like that. After all, he might not have created the framework in which we functioned, but he was still our ruler, and there were a lot of things wrong that he needed to fix.

All of which takes time.

Sighing, I handed my finished plate to one of the kitchen staff, then headed back up the steps and toward the West Wing. I knew that the Chief Mage had been busy wading through the administrative mess Argon Chartis, the former Director of the Mage's Guild, had left behind, and that he was strapped for time. Yes, it wasn't right that he was neglecting my tutelage as a mage, but I couldn't have it both ways if I wanted him to fix what was wrong in the city.

Maybe, but that's no reason he can't give you some time off to go and hunt bounties for the Guild.

I fought against the urge to gnash my teeth, knowing that walking into the training room angry was only going to make this evening worse. But that was the whole crux of the situation – I wouldn't be so angry about his lack of time to train me if he'd just let me do my job as an enforcer so I could earn some money.

I pushed open the training room door, then bit my lip when I saw the open, rectangular space was empty. Checking my watch, I realized that I'd gotten here a few minutes early, so I went and sat cross-legged in the middle of the floor to meditate while I waited for him. No, I wasn't going to give up on my crusade to make Iannis let me go back to work, but tonight I knew I needed to swallow my pill and keep my mouth shut about it. I'd already pissed him off enough.

Closing my eyes, I placed my hands on the insides of my thighs, then drew a deep breath in through my nostrils. I held it for a moment, then let it out, and tried to visualize my anger and frustration exiting my body along with the breath. It was an exercise Roanas had taught me, and one that he'd found useful in mitigating his own emotions – an important skill for an investigator. I'd never been as good as it as he was – I'd always preferred the physical aspects of Kan Zao, the Garaian martial art he'd taught me, over the mental ones.

I scented the Chief Mage's approach before I heard his soft footsteps in the hall – his fragrance of sandalwood, musk and magic was unmistakable. My heart began to beat a little faster as the door opened, but I forced myself to take another deep breath and calm down. I didn't give a damn if he saw me meditating on the floor – at least he'd know I was trying to control myself.

But when his robes swished across the floor in front of me, I couldn't keep my eyes closed any longer. Nerves prickling, I lifted my head to meet his eyes, wondering what I would see. His face was as impassive as ever, but to my surprise there was no ire in his eyes – just contemplation as he gazed down at me.

"Come," he finally said, holding out a hand.

I hesitated. "We're not using the training room today?"

"No. I have something else in mind."

I took his hand, and warmth flowed down my arm as he wrapped his strong fingers around me. He pulled me up in one effortless motion, and I wondered, not for the first time, about what kind of body lay beneath those blue and gold robes. He was strong, stronger than a man who relied so heavily on magic should be, and I was curious as to just why that was.

As soon as I was on my feet, the Chief Mage dropped my hand, then turned to leave, his robes swirling about behind him.

My hand tingled as I followed, and though I itched to ask where we were going, I decided to keep my mouth shut. If he'd wanted me to know, he would have told me already, and I'd decided to do my best not to be annoying tonight.

I expected Iannis to take me somewhere else in the Palace, but to my surprise we headed out through the side entrance, where carriages and steamcars dropped off their deliveries. A horse-drawn carriage waited for us, and the driver hopped down from his seat to open the door, greeting the Chief Mage with a reverence and respect I'd never been able to manage.

"Okay," I said as the carriage rumbled off, its wooden wheels bumping over the cobblestones as it made its way onto the smoother, paved road. "I can't take it anymore. Where are we going?"

Iannis's violet eyes gleamed in the dark interior of the cabin. "Somewhere I should have taken you from the very beginning of your apprenticeship."

I tried to get him to tell me more, but he ignored my attempts to pry information out of him, so I sighed and settled back against the suede upholstery. The carriage took us up Firegate Road, and I leaned forward a little so I could look out the window as we drove across the bridge. The huge red towers soared above us, and using my eyes I traced the cables that stretched between them on either side of the carriage. Beyond the cables, I could see Prison Isle, the watchtower attached to the compound gleaming brightly in the darkness. The moon shining overhead was brighter still, already visible even though the sky was streaked with the lingering pastels of the dying sun. It was only half-full, but I felt the tug of its power. Shifters had a close relationship with the moon – Magorah actually meant 'moon's child' in an ancient language – and when it was full we were able to shift faster and more frequently than usual.

Once across the bridge, the carriage turned onto a winding

road that I recognized as the one that led up to Hawk Hill. My interest was instantly piqued – Hawk Hill was an excellent vantage point from which to view Solantha and the Firegate Bridge, but it was also frequented by mages, and wards at the top of the hill prevented anyone else from going past a certain point. Looking down at my hands, I wondered if I could breach them now, the way I'd temporarily breached the wards around Solantha Palace in order to save my cousin Rylan from his botched attempt to rescue me a few months ago.

But then, I had a feeling I wouldn't need to force my way past these wards, not with the Chief Mage at my side.

The driver took us to the top of the hill, then parked in a safe, level spot to wait for us while we did... whatever it was we were doing. The wind tugged at my curls as I disembarked, bringing a faint touch of sea salt with it, and even more strongly, the burnt-sugar scent of magic. The hairs on my arms prickled at the enormous amount of magical energy here – I was unprepared for how strong it was, and I'd never felt anything like it anywhere else. Nervous, I turned my head to glance back at the bay. I had a feeling that whatever the Chief Mage was about to show me would change my life in some way, and I'd already been through so many changes in the last two months. Was I ready for another?

"Come." Iannis's voice pulled me from my thoughts. "Much as I would love to stand here and enjoy the view, my time is limited."

Right. I followed Iannis up the hill, the soft grass rustling beneath my boots. The scent of magic grew even stronger, and after about ten paces he held up a hand.

"Repeat after me," he said, and then he spoke a Word.

It took me three tries to get it right, but when I did, the air in front of us shimmered, like heat waves were suddenly rising from the grass. I gasped as a domed building suddenly appeared out of nowhere, and took an involuntary step back. It towered above us, crafted of some kind of strange blue stone that shimmered in the moonlight, with round, stained glass windows set into the walls.

"What is this place?"

"A temple." The Chief Mage glanced back at me, amusement flickering in his violet eyes. "I didn't realize you were frightened of buildings."

"I'm not frightened," I snapped, folding my arms across my chest. "I'm just not used to fifty foot structures appearing out of thin air, is all." Holy shit, the mages had been hiding a *temple* here the whole time? What for? I wasn't aware they even had a place of worship. I stared up at the structure, still flabbergasted that this thing existed. Golden runes shimmered along the edges of the dome, the windows, and the arch that framed the front door. The scent of magic here was thicker than in Solantha Palace, which was really saying something since the Mages Guild was housed there.

"Come," the Chief Mage said again, gesturing impatiently. "Let's go inside."

"What is this temple *for*?" I asked as we approached the doorway. The wooden door looked heavy and imposing, but it swung open on its own, and I had a sense that the building was welcoming us inside. Which was weird, because buildings weren't sentient as far as I knew.

"It's where we worship the Creator," the Chief Mage said simply.

We stepped inside, and I stood still for a long moment, taking in the space. The torches lining the walls helped illuminate the rounded space, as well as a circular skylight set into the top of the vaulted dome, and decorative pillars that lined the inside of the temple. But all of this paled in comparison to the sight of the enormous white statue that dominated the center of the temple. The sculpture stood at least thirty feet tall, carved out of pure white marble into the shape of a woman. Her long hair was unbound, and a set of robes flowed around her willowy figure. A large book lay cradled in one arm, and the other was outstretched, revealing an open palm facing upward from which a blue-white flame blazed.

"Who is that?" I asked, pointing up at the woman.

The Chief Mage gently laid his palm over my outstretched hand and pushed it down. "It's rude to point," he said quietly, and I stared -- he was looking up at the statue with a reverent expression I'd never seen before.

"This is Resinah," he said, still looking up at the statue. "She was the first mage brought into existence by the Creator, and was endowed with the power to transform humans, animals and matter. She chose twelve disciples to share her power with, and it is from Resinah and her disciples that our lineage as mages springs."

"The Creator?" I echoed, staring up at the statue again. "You mean Magorah?"

A frown briefly touched the Chief Mage's face. "You may call him by a different name, just as humans believe in the Ur-God, but I believe we all worship the same deity. It's just a matter of which interpretation is the correct one," he allowed. "I am not here to invalidate your faith, Miss Baine, but Resinah is a very important part of our heritage, and all mages learn her teachings very early on."

"How come Resinah and her disciples are never mentioned in any of the public school text books?" I demanded. I wasn't devout, not by any means, but I'd always grown up with the idea of Magorah in my head and heart, and in His place of worship it was taught that mages were simply the instruments He used to create shifters, and that we were His favorite children.

"We are very... private, about our religious beliefs. The teachings of Resinah are not intended for outsiders, and are of little use to non-mages in any case. Additionally, it was decided long ago that rather than try to indoctrinate other races into our teachings, that we would allow you to keep your own religions. Not all mages agreed with this decision, but so far we have all abided by it," he added dryly.

"Okay." I glanced up at the statue again, wondering if Resinah had really looked like that. She had a stern but classically beautiful face, and the book in one hand and the flame in the other seemed to emphasize knowledge and power equally. I found it interesting that she was a woman; in our faith the first shifter had been a female as well – Taili the Wolf. Females were the ones primarily responsible for procreation, so I supposed it made sense that Magorah would choose females through which to do His work. Much as I wanted to deny it, a holy presence permeated the air of this temple. It was like the presence I'd felt in Magorah's temple in Shiftertown, except that here the air was also heavily laced with magic. Maybe Magorah and Iannis's Creator really *were* one and the same, as he'd said.

"Do you come here often?" I wondered aloud. "Do mages have a worship schedule or something, or do you just come and go as you please?"

"There are certain times of the year that we gather, but mostly we come and go of our own accord, generally when we are seeking guidance."

"Does she talk to you then?" The idea was half-absurd, half-intriguing – I'd felt Magorah's presence at times and thought I'd heard His voice once or twice in moments of need, but I'd never out-and-out had a conversation with him.

"She's not a conversationalist, but she will provide guidance in moments of true need." Iannis stared up at the statue, some undefinable emotion glimmering in his violet eyes. "Not very long ago I came to Resinah seeking advice on how to deal with a rather terrible dilemma. Her wisdom encouraged me to show mercy in a situation where the law would suggest otherwise."

"Huh." I stared at the Chief Mage, wondering just what kind of situation had been so untenable that he'd sought out advice from his deity rather than enforce the laws he governed so strictly with. But I could tell from the look in his eye that he wasn't going to say any more about it, so I didn't press.

"So did you bring me here just to show me the temple?" I asked, wanting to change the subject. "Or is there more?"

"There is more." The Chief Mage sighed a little as I turned to face him again. "I don't condone your behavior in my office today, nor your absence from the Mages Guild this morning... but I do acknowledge that your education has been lackluster so far. I realized that you have not been given any of the education most mages already receive from their families by the time they begin an apprenticeship, and that because of your unusual power level I may have been harder on you than I should." He reached into his sleeve, and pulled out a heavy, leather-bound tome. "This is a copy of the *Residah*, the book of scripture that holds Resinah's teachings. Every mage reads this book early on, and it's time you did so as well."

"You really need to teach me that trick sometime." I took the tome from him gingerly, running my hand across the runes carved in relief across the teal-colored leather. "Being able to pull objects out of thin air would be a useful talent for someone like me, you know." I'd decided that Iannis's sleeve itself wasn't enchanted, otherwise he'd have to move all the stuff he stored in there to a different robe each time he changed. Maybe he had some kind of mystical air pocket that hovered near his forearm.

"I can imagine." Iannis's lips twitched into a rare smile, softening his stern features and drawing my attention to how handsome he was. "When you finish reading this, I will teach you the spell."

"Now *that's* motivation." I glanced down at the heavy book in my hand, not so much because I wanted to look at it again but because warmth was spreading through my cheeks, and I didn't want Iannis to pick up on it. I'd thought that between moving out of the Palace and seeing him so infrequently, his effect on me would lessen, but the butterflies in my stomach were just as active as they always were when I caught brief flashes of humor, compassion or heat from him. The fact that we were alone here didn't help matters.

I raised my head as a thought occurred to me. "Why is no one else here?" I asked. "Don't other mages come here to umm... worship? Or whatever it is you do here?" And wouldn't there at least be attendants or something?

"Yes, but I asked that the temple be cleared for our visit this evening," Iannis said. "I didn't want other mages to distract you."

He sent them away for me. More warmth filled my chest, followed by a healthy dose of shame, and I looked away.

"I'm sorry."

"Hmm?" For the first time I could recall, confusion entered Iannis's voice. "What for?"

"For not thanking you." Tears pricked at the corners of my eyes, and I blinked them away before turning to look him in the eye – I was *not* going to cry in front of the Chief Mage. "For sparing my life, for taking me on as your apprentice, for everything you've taught me so far... I've never thanked you for any of it. And I'm sorry."

"Well, that must have been incredibly difficult for you to say." The surprise on Iannis's face melted into another small smile. "If I didn't know better, Miss Baine, I would say that you're maturing."

"Hey, it's a process." I stuck out my tongue. I might have been twenty-four years old, but shifters lived for hundreds of years, and as far as I was concerned that meant my brain still had a little ways to go to catch up with how old I looked.

"Indeed. I'd hoped that between studying Resinah's scripture and your increased exposure to other mages that you'd begin taking after your other half more. It would seem that it's working." He smirked a little.

"Soooo... does this mean that you'll give me time off in the mornings now? You know, so I can study this book?" I grinned, knowing he would see right through my ploy, but the tension between us had lightened significantly, and I figured I'd take a shot.

To my surprise, a thoughtful glimmer entered Iannis's eyes. "I would be willing to allow you to come in an hour later to give you time to read in the mornings," he allowed. "But rest assured you'll be quizzed at the beginning of every lesson, so if I find you've been abusing the privilege I will take it away."

"Ugh." I rolled my eyes. "You know, at this rate I may as well just take out one of those interest-free loans Sandin Federal Bank is offering. I need to start earning money again."

"Interest-free loans?" Instantly, all the levity vanished from the Chief Mage's expression. "What are you talking about?"

"Sandin Federal Bank is offering such loans specifically for shifters," I said carefully, wary of the dangerous tone that had entered his voice. "I heard about it at a diner in Shiftertown today. Apparently a lot of shifters have accepted them, and they seem to be pretty happy about it too. I figured I may as well take advantage."

"Absolutely not."

"Excuse me?" I stiffened at the authoritative tone in his voice.

"Under no circumstances should you accept the loan from Sandin Federal Bank," Iannis said sternly. "Loans of that sort are highly suspect, and the terms they are offering are likely to be illegal. They could cause you great financial hardship in the future."

"Oh." I deflated momentarily, and then stood up straight again. "Well how do you know the terms are illegal? Isn't it worth checking out at least?" I wasn't actually keen on going into debt, but the rebel in me was chafing at the idea that I couldn't at least consider the terms.

"Terms that look too good to be true usually are. There is no such thing as free money, and the fine print will likely have some caveat, such as interest rates kicking in after a certain period of time. But I suppose it's worth finding out exactly what the fine print says." Iannis tapped his triangular chin, his eyes narrowing. "In fact, I think that's exactly what you should do."

"Huh?" I gaped at him as if he'd suddenly grown a second head.

"Yes." Iannis nodded in satisfaction, more to himself than to me, I think. "I'd like you to investigate the terms of the loan, find out how long the bank has been offering it, and if there have been any repercussions on the shifters who have taken the money. I would do it myself, but as you know I am leaving for the Convention soon and Fenris and I are both pressed for time."

"Right." That damned Convention again. "When exactly am I going to have time to do this? In case you haven't realized this, banks are closed in the evenings."

"I will allow you to take the next three mornings off to conduct the investigation," he relented. "I realize you will need more time in your schedule, and this is more important than your routine duties at the Mages Guild. But make no mistake; if I don't have any results from you by the end of the week, there *will* be consequences."

"Oh believe me, I'll have your results for you." I grinned, and if Iannis hadn't been standing in front of me I would have danced around the room, sacred temple be damned. Investigating the bank seemed simple enough, and three days was enough time for me to do it while also looking into Sillara's murder with Inspector Lakin. After all, who said a girl couldn't multitask?

7

*B*y the time I got back to my apartment in Rowanville, it was late in the evening, and long shadows stretched across the room, silhouetted by the moonlight that streamed through my bay window. I flicked on the light, then hung up my leather jacket before heading toward my kitchen to scrounge up something to eat. I'd considered hounding Lakin, but the *Residah* called to me, inviting me to open its pages. I figured I might as well get started on it tonight to free up my morning for my investigation.

Settling down on the couch with my back against the armrest and my knees drawn up, I made quick work of a bowl of sausage and potatoes. With a full belly and a satisfied sigh, I propped the book up against my thighs and began to skim through the table of contents so I could see what was in this thing. A chapter called 'The Mage's Code of Honor' jumped out at me, and I flipped to it, curious to see what sort of standard Resinah expected of mages back in her day.

I. *Magic is an extension of oneself. Every charm made and*

spell cast is a reflection on one's soul. Treat all requests to perform magic with this in mind.

2. *Magic is a gift given to us by the Creator, and must be treated with proper reverence. The possessor of magic is not a god, but rather an extension of one. Use magic to protect the weak, rather than take advantage of them.*

3. *In order to properly use the gift of magic, one must agree not to commit any acts of magic that go against the Creator's tenets, including, but not limited to:*

- *The murder of another mage or human*
- *The exploitation of humans and other lesser beings through magical means*
- *The performance of a spell on another mage or human that affects their mind or body without their express permission, with self-defense as an exception*

I STOPPED THERE, pursing my lips as indignation burned in my chest. The mages had blown the third tenet right out of the water when they'd created shifters. I wondered just how many of the original humans the mages used to create shifters had participated willingly. Had any? Just how sacred did the mages hold the *Residah*?

The telephone on the kitchen counter rang, interrupting my train of thought. Annoyed, I set the book on the coffee table, then got up to answer it. Much as I would have rather ignored it, I didn't get phone calls very often, and I was curious as to who it was.

"Hello?"

"Sunaya Baine." A deep, hoarse voice sounded from the

other end. "You should stop sticking your whiskers into matters that don't concern you."

"What are you talking about?" My entire body stiffened at the veiled threat, and my ears strained, trying to identify the voice on the other line.

"I think you know what I'm talking about." The voice turned slightly smug. "You wouldn't want to end up like poor Sillara, would you?"

"I'm a lot tougher than Sillara was," I growled, finally understanding. This asshole was trying to get me to stop helping Lakin with his investigation. "Who the fuck are you, anyway?" There was a barely audible strain in his speech that told me it wasn't the speaker's natural voice.

"If you're not concerned about your own safety, then be concerned for your family." The voice turned darker. "Meddle in our affairs, and they will pay the price."

I opened my mouth to tell him that my family and I didn't give two shits about each other, but the line disconnected, leaving me with nothing to shout at but a dial tone. Frustrated, I slammed the receiver back down into the cradle. This wasn't the first time I'd received a threatening phone call, but they usually involved my own hide, not someone else's.

Sighing, I returned to my position on the couch, but I couldn't bring myself to touch the book on the table. Instead, my mind wrestled with the phone call. Whoever the caller was, they must be involved in the kidnappings, but what had alerted them to my involvement? Was it because I'd visited the Enforcer's Guild today and demanded Sillara's files? Dammit, but I should have found a way to keep a lower profile during my visit.

I ground my teeth together at the idea of another traitor in the Enforcer's Guild. The last time, it had been Deputy Talcon who'd been pulling strings from the inside – he'd been in league with

Petros Yantz, and it was because of his interference that the silver poisonings weren't properly investigated. I'd killed him in self-defense when he and Yantz had kidnapped me and taken me to Yantz's mansion to find out what I knew about their operation, which to my frustration had been precious little. I'd already known that they were using *kalois*, a special herb from a foreign continent that kept shifters from detecting the deadly silver slipped into their food and drink, and into the drugs that were being distributed throughout Shiftertown. But we hadn't yet figured out the endgame, or the identity of the mastermind behind it. Yantz and Talcon had only referred to him as 'the Benefactor,' and implied that their operation was merely the beginning of something much larger.

Whatever Sillara had been involved with, it probably had something to do with this larger plan. And I had a bad feeling that even if we figured out what it was, the Benefactor would still be miles ahead of us.

MORNING SUNLIGHT STRUCK my closed eyelids, and I opened them to find that I was still on the couch, where I'd eventually fallen asleep after a restless night. I'd spent the better part of my night staring at the ceiling as I tried to come up with theories about who the caller could have been, and also about whether or not I should warn my "family" that they were in danger. On the one hand, my aunt Mafiela and I hated each other, and if someone took her out I certainly wouldn't lose any sleep over it. But there were innocent cubs in the Jaguar Clan that an outsider could loosely consider to be my family, and I didn't want their blood anywhere near my hands.

In the end, I grabbed a shower and a change of clothes, then rode my bike over to my aunt's house in Shiftertown. She lived in the upper crust section of town, where rows of tri-colored terraced houses nestled side-by-side like a set of painted eggs in a carton, though nowhere near as fragile. My aunt wasn't the cheerful type though; she'd painted her house a dark purple, and the shutters and roof tiles were a complementary but boring dark grey. Not even the flowers nestled in the beds out front offered any of bright colors – they were beautiful, but pure white.

I left my steambike on the curb, then trotted up the steps and banged on the front door with a heavy brass knocker molded into the shape of a jaguar head. A few moments later, a blond jaguar shifter dressed in a suit and tie answered the door, his yellow eyes already narrowed in disapproval.

"Hey, Hennis." I greeted my aunt's butler casually, as if he weren't looking down his nose at me like I was a spot of dung on his shiny shoes. Damn, but he could give the mages lessons on how to be a supercilious asshole. "Is my aunt home?"

"I'm afraid Chieftain Baine is not accepting visitors at this moment." Hennis's lips thinned. "Perhaps I could take a message."

"Sorry, but this isn't a social call." I lifted my wrist, flashing the enforcer's shield that hung from my leather bracelet in the shape of a small bronze charm. "I'm here on official business."

"Very well. Please wait here."

He shut the door in my face, and I sighed, resigned to waiting on the front porch of the house I'd lived in for a good portion of my childhood. Though Aunt Mafiela had disapproved of my mother's illegitimate pregnancy, she'd loved my mother all the same and had allowed us both to live with her. This house had many good memories from when my mother was alive, as well as plenty of dark ones from the two years I'd lived here without her.

If I'd been any other enforcer, Hennis would have invited me to wait in the receiving parlor. But because I was the black sheep, the hated relation, I was stuck out on the porch. Oh well, at least it was summer, and early enough in the day that the temperature was tolerable.

The door opened once more, and my lovely aunt glared at me from behind the threshold. She couldn't have looked less like me, dressed in a ruffled white blouse and high-waisted grey pants that showed off her slender figure, her blonde hair swept back from her diamond-shaped face into an elegant bun. The end of her nose was slightly tilted up, like mine, and her eyes were the same size and shape. But her irises were yellow, like the majority of the Jaguar Clan, whereas mine were bottle green – just one more thing to set me apart from everyone else.

"By Magorah, Sunaya. What do you want?" she demanded, her eyes glimmering with annoyance. "It's barely midmorning!" Jaguars were notoriously nocturnal, so for Mafiela it was like I'd come knocking at seven in the morning.

"Oh I'm sorry, did I disturb your beauty sleep?" I snapped, raking her with a sneer. I couldn't help it – everything about the woman set me on edge. "I know how much you need it." It was a lie of course – Mafiela was beautiful, with her sharp cheekbones, thickly-lashed eyes and generous mouth.

A flush spread across those sharp cheekbones, and she peeled back her lips to snarl at me, fangs exposed. "I don't have to take this kind of abuse from you. If you don't have anything important to say, you can leave." She made to shut the door.

"Oh stop it." I stuck my boot on the brass threshold, preventing her from closing the door. "I'm here because a threat was made against your family recently."

Mafiela's eyes flashed. "A threat? What kind of threat?"

"It was a little vague," I admitted, shoving my hands into my pockets. "But I got a phone call last night from someone telling me that if I didn't drop an investigation, that they would come after my family." I curled my lips back into a sneer of my own.

"They hung up the phone before I had a chance to tell them I don't have a family."

"Hmph." Mafiela turned her nose up at me. "Well if you think I'm going to thank you for delivering the warning, you can think again. After all, it's your fault if we're being threatened in the first place."

"Oh gee, I didn't think of that. Thanks for bestowing such great wisdom upon me by pointing it out."

Mafiela snarled at me. "You always were such a smart-ass."

"Yeah, and you always were a crotchety old puss." I sneered at her.

"How dare you!" Mafiela's cheeks mottled, her yellow eyes blazing. "Get off my property, you ungrateful kit! And don't come back. I don't want you or your filthy magic anywhere near my clan."

"Oh don't worry," I snapped, tossing my head. "I have no intention of setting foot into the cesspit you call a home ever again. Enjoy the rest of your day, *Chieftain* Baine."

Fuming, I hopped down the porch steps and got back on my bike, wanting to put as much distance between myself and that horrid house as possible. By Magorah, but couldn't the woman at least *pretend* to be civil? And people wondered where I got my bitchiness from. Shaking my head, I urged my bike down the hill and toward the Shifter Courier's offices, which were only a few minutes away. I doubted the editor would be any more cooperative than my aunt, but I was a lot more confident I would actually get something productive done by visiting him.

The Shifter Courier looked a lot more dilapidated than the round, pristine white structure that housed the Herald in Maintown. It was a tall, narrow rectangular building, maybe five stories high, but each of those stories was small, maybe one and a half times the size of my one-bedroom apartment. The ornate molding that lined the facade of the building was crumbling in places, and the windows were filthy, several of them even boarded up. Guess they really had fallen on hard times.

I walked into the lobby, which didn't look much better than the outside – there were framed newspapers from the Courier's better days hanging from the walls, but the white paint behind them was flaking off in places, and the grey carpet beneath my feet was threadbare. A female rabbit shifter sat behind a rickety looking reception desk, her slender fingers tapping away at a typewriter. Her powder-blue eyes widened at my approach.

"H-hello," she stammered, tucking a wisp of pale brown hair behind her ear. I pegged her as a new hire, and gathered she probably wasn't used to visitors. "How can I help you?" Her small, rounded nose twitched nervously, and I imagined that if she was in beast form her whiskers would be quivering.

"My name is Sunaya Baine, and I'm with the Enforcer's Guild." I held up my wrist so that she could see my bracelet. "I need to speak with your Chief Editor."

"Oh." The receptionist bit her lip, exposing two large front teeth – a common rabbit shifter characteristic, even in human form. "I'm not sure he's available."

"Well if he's not, he needs to make himself available." I tried to curb the annoyance in my voice, wanting to take pity on her, but I wasn't going to let this rabbity female turn me away – I needed answers. "You do know that if he refuses to speak to me that's considered obstruction of justice, and I'm within my rights to arrest him and take him with me to the Enforcer's Guild for questioning. I'm sure your boss wouldn't want that, would he?"

"No!" she squeaked, her eyes widening. "No, of course not. Let me just tell him you're here. One moment."

She snatched up the phone on her desk, and I waited patiently for her to speak to the Chief Editor. "He said he'll see you in his office," she said when she hung up. "It's on the third floor, room –"

"I know where it is," I interrupted, already moving past her to the stairwell on her left – I'd been here before. There was an elevator, but the thing was so rickety I didn't dare trust it, so I trotted up the three flights of stairs to the executive offices.

Of course, that sounded a lot more impressive than it was – the floors were small, and there were maybe three offices total in this space. Faron Gor, the Courier's Chief Editor, had a corner office that boasted some of the only windows that weren't filthy or boarded up, so he had a decent view of the city from his desk. Like the lobby, his walls were covered in old framed newspaper clippings, and his frayed carpet was in desperate need of replacement. The space was cramped, taken up by shelves and file cabinets, with room for only a single wooden chair in front of his desk.

"Enforcer Baine!" Faron exclaimed as soon as he noticed me waiting at his open doorway. He stood up quickly, and rounded the desk to greet me. He was a wolf shifter, with dark coarse brown hair cropped close to his square head, rugged features, and a stocky frame. The grey suit he wore looked cheap, but clean. "Please, come in." He held out a hand for me to shake.

I blinked, caught off guard by his genuine manner, but I shook his hand. "Thanks for agreeing to see me on such short notice."

"Of course." He sat down behind his desk again, and I made myself as comfortable as possible in the wooden visitor's chair. "What can I do for the Enforcer's Guild today?"

"I'm here regarding a series of kidnappings that have occurred over the last year." I pulled a notebook from the inside of my jacket pocket, where I'd scribbled down the names from Sillara's list, and read them off. "Do any of them sound familiar to you?"

An uncomfortable look flashed across Faron's face. "They do, yes."

I scowled at the admission. "Then why were so many of them unreported by the media? If you knew about them, surely your reporters did too, or you would have told one of them."

Faron sighed. "I wanted to print those stories, I really did. They would have been good for business. But there was pressure from one of our major advertisers not to do so. They said that if we did they would take their business elsewhere, and we caved because we would have to close our doors without their income."

"I see." I wanted to berate Faron for giving in so easily, but given the precarious state of his business, I couldn't blame him too much. His first priority was keeping his ship afloat, and if that meant catering to his advertisers then that's what he had to do. "You know, that kind of suspicious activity is really something you should report to the Guild."

Faron gave me a dry look. "It would just get filed away in the archives. With no bounty attached to the case, I doubt anyone would have a look."

"Yeah, but at least the report would have left a trail and it could have saved me some time." But I sighed, knowing the truth of his words – that was one of the major flaws with our system. "Can you at least give me the name of the advertiser now?"

"Of course. They're called the Butcher's Block." He scribbled the name onto a piece of paper along with a phone number and handed it to me. "Is there anything else I can do for you?"

The hopeful look on his face made me pause. "Should there be?"

His broad shoulders sagged a little. "Well I was hoping you were coming to me with something I could use for a story."

A twinge of pity in my chest had me sighing again. "I don't have anything concrete on these current murders yet, and I'm not really in the loop on anything else right now. But if I get hold of anything I can share with you, I'll give you a call, okay?"

"I'd appreciate that." Faron hesitated. "There's something else you should know."

"And what would that be?" I asked, my senses tingling at the tone in his voice.

"One of my reporters, Nevin Rindar, disappeared about two months ago. He was the reporter I would have assigned to write the stories. I filed a report with the Enforcer's Guild, but they have yet to figure out what happened to him."

"I'll look into it." If he'd only disappeared two months ago, he wouldn't have been in Roanas's files, which explained why his name hadn't come up. "Do you have an address for his residence? It would save me a trip to the Guild."

"Of course." Faron wrote it down on another piece of paper and handed it to me. "I really hope he's alright. He is a good reporter."

"I hope so too." But I didn't have a good feeling about it. I vaguely remembered Nevin – I'd had to deal with him once or twice – and I suspected that whatever had happened to the others had befallen him as well. "I'll let you know when I find out what happened."

"Thank you." Faron paused, his eyes shifting away for a moment before he met my gaze. "I know that we posted some uncomplimentary things in the paper about you when your... heritage...became public. I want to apologize for that."

I shrugged. "You were just doing your job. I'm the Jaguar Clan's outcast, and the Chieftain's niece on top of it. Can't imagine you've had a juicier story in a long time." Old resentment bubbled up inside me at the reminder of those stories, but I pushed them down – there was no point in bringing it up.

"That's true. Our sales skyrocketed during your hearing and imprisonment, I must admit." Faron smiled briefly. "A lot of the shifters in the community don't know how to feel about you, Sunaya. They want to hate you because you're half-mage, and there's a part of me that understands that. But I know how hard you fought to solve the silver murders. You're one of the good ones."

"Thanks." I smiled, any resentment I felt toward the Courier evaporating. My nose told me his words were sincere, and they warmed me. "I'll be in touch."

I went to Lakin's house next, and banged on the door for several minutes until he answered. His steambike was parked right out front, so I knew he was home, and damned if I was going to come back later. I didn't have a whole lot of time left until I had to report to the Mages Guild, so if I didn't see him now I wouldn't see him until tonight, if that.

"Oh for Magorah's sake!" Lakin finally shouted from the back of the house. "Just give me a moment, would you?"

I grinned at the sound of footsteps stomping across the floor-boards, and a few seconds later, Lakin flung open the door. My eyebrows jumped as I took a good look at him – his short blond hair was sticking out in all directions, his lower jaw was covered in stubble, and he wore only a pair of loose drawstring pants that hung low on his hips, revealing his lean, muscular torso. His chest was lightly dusted with blond hair that trailed over his abdomen and disappeared beneath the waistband of his pants, drawing attention to the v-cut of his abdomen.

"Well good morning." I waggled my eyebrows at him. "Do you normally answer the door like this, or is it just when the ladies come calling?"

"Sunaya?" A bewildered look crossed Lakin's sleep-creased face, and to my surprise, he blushed. "Sorry, I wasn't expecting you. Come in, come in."

Bemused, I followed him inside, watching the self-conscious way he ran a hand through his hair. Shifters as a general rule weren't modest, so I doubted Lakin was concerned that I'd just seen him half-naked. Maybe it was just that he looked so disheveled. I guess if my hair looked like that I'd be self-conscious too.

"Do you want coffee or anything?" Lakin asked, leading me into his kitchen. It was small but cozy, with the sink, counter and cabinets taking up the far side of the space, and the refrigerator and a small, wooden table and chair set on the other. "I just bought a new roast yesterday."

"No, I'm good." I wasn't a huge coffee fan to begin with.

"Great. Let me just... can I just grab a shirt? I'm a little cold."

"Uh, sure." I arched a brow as he darted out of the kitchen. Shifters didn't easily get cold, and it was the middle of summer. But I wasn't about to call him on it – if wearing a shirt around me made him more comfortable then I wasn't going to object. I wanted his full attention, after all. Bored, I fiddled with the cord of the red telephone that sat atop the table, twisting it around my finger as I waited for Lakin to return.

When Lakin finally came back, I could see he'd done more than throw a shirt on. I arched a brow at the sight of his wet, neatly combed hair and the pair of jeans he'd traded his sweatpants for, but again, I said nothing.

"So," he said, clasping his hands together as he rested his forearms atop the table. "What's going on?'

"I came to give you an update on the case."

Lakin's brows arched. "Have you?" His lips twitched a little. "I didn't realize you'd been working on it without me."

"Yeah, well I couldn't stop thinking about it after I left so I decided to do a little more digging." I told him about my visit to the Shifter Courier this morning, then pulled out the scrap of paper with the advertiser's name and number on it. "I was thinking you might want to call The Butcher's Block and question the contact. They don't have a local office so a phone call might save some time."

"How nice of you." Lakin took the paper from me, still frowning. "It's good to know I'm allowed to participate in my own investigation."

My spine stiffened. "Are you saying that you would rather not have my help?" I asked, offended at his tone.

"No, no, of course not." Lakin let out a huff. "I'm just frustrated that you made some headway while I ended up chasing my tail for most of yesterday."

"Oh." My scowl softened into a more sympathetic expression. "None of your interviews panned out?"

"Not a one so far." Lakin shook his head. "Sillara's partner told me that she'd come home to find her door unlocked not long after Sillara's death, but she hadn't noticed anything missing so she figured she'd just forgotten to lock up when she'd left. None of the families I've interviewed so far have told me anything helpful, and several of the missing shifters had moved to Solantha from outside Canalo. Their families, if any, will be hard to track down."

"Well, hopefully we'll get something helpful now. Why don't you make that phone call?"

Lakin picked up the phone, then dialed the number on the piece of paper. We listened to the shrill ring tone for a couple of seconds, and then a receptionist answered in a cheery voice. Lakin asked for Borin Tate, the advertising rep Faron said had made the call.

"I'm sorry," the receptionist said after a moment. *"But there is no Borin Tate in the company register."*

"There isn't?" Lakin scowled. "How long has he been gone?"

"To my knowledge no one by that name has never worked here." The receptionist paused. *"Is there someone else I can direct your call to?"*

Lakin sighed in disgust. "Your current advertising representative would be a good start."

"One moment please."

Lakin gave me a look as the receptionist transferred him. "This isn't going well so far," he muttered.

"Yeah well, let's see what this guy has to say." But I bit my lip, privately agreeing with him.

"Hello, this is Wilam Randor," a male answered. *"Can I help you?"*

"Yes, hello." Lakin's voice was smooth and professional. "My name is Inspector Lakin, and I'm calling from Solantha's Shiftertown regarding an investigation. Do you have a moment?"

"Certainly." The man sounded surprised, but polite. *"How can I be of assistance?"*

"It's come to my attention that your company recently threatened to pull their advertising dollars from the Shifter Courier. Is this true?"

"Why no," the man insisted. *"The Shifter Courier brings us a significant amount of business each year. I wouldn't think to do such a thing."*

"I see. And how long have you been employed in your current position?"

"Three years."

"Okay. Have you ever used a temp, such as on sick leave or vacation, in the past year?"

"Oh no," the man said emphatically. *"Whenever I take time off my supervisor takes over for me. We don't trust that kind of thing to temporary employees."*

"Alright. Thank you very much for your time."

Lakin hung up the phone, then glared at the receiver. "Another dead end."

"Yeah." My shoulders slumped. If the person who'd made the phone call wasn't an employee of the company, there was no way for us to track them down. The incident had happened far too long ago, in any case.

"Oh wait. There's one more thing." I dug out the other piece of paper Faron had given me and gave it to Lakin. "The Chief Editor also told me that one of his reporters, the one who would normally be in charge of writing up the disappearances, has disappeared himself recently."

"Huh." Lakin's eyes lit with interest as he stared down at the address. "Say, that house is right up the street from here, a few blocks away. What do you say we check it out now?"

"That's exactly what I was thinking."

Lakin donned his leather coat, and we walked over to Nevin's house, leaving our steambikes parked outside Lakin's residence. Like Lakin's house, it was a small, one story dwelling, but unlike Lakin's place there was a distinct air of neglect hanging about it. The grass on the front yard was nearly a foot high, the planters were empty of flowers, and there was the faintest whiff of rotting garbage.

"Ugh." I pinched my nose as we approached the front door, the smell getting stronger. "How has no one come to investigate by now? This whole block is full of shifters. Surely they would have come over to complain about this stench."

Lakin shrugged. "The smell's not too bad from the street. He probably wasn't incredibly friendly with his neighbors, and nobody cared enough about the smell to bother with it."

"Yeah, well looks like garbage wasn't his only problem." I looked over at the overflowing mailbox hanging from the exterior wall to the left of the door. Grabbing a few letters, I noticed they were postmarked from the end of April. "I get the feeling the postman stopped delivering weeks ago ."

The front door was locked, so Lakin fished a set of lock picks from one of his pockets. I arched a brow as he jimmied one of them into the locks, and seconds later the mechanism clicked open.

"Didn't know Inspectors were allowed to do that kind of thing." I could pick locks with the best of them, but since I went after wanted criminals, breaking into their houses was a little different from doing it to someone who as far as we knew was innocent.

Lakin snorted. "You wouldn't believe how many times I've had to do this," he said as the door swung open.

The rotting garbage stench was even stronger on the inside, and as we quickly discovered, came from the kitchen trash and the refrigerator, where months-old supplies of meat and dairy lay wasting away, covered with green and black mold. Gagging, I quickly closed the refrigerator and moved out of the room, wanting to get myself away from the awful smell as fast as possible.

"Lakin?" I called as I moved into the living room. Unlike Lakin's it was fully furnished, but the surfaces were covered in a layer of dust. This guy definitely hadn't been home in awhile, probably since he'd stopped showing up to work.

"In here," Lakin called, and I followed the sound of his voice into Nevin's bedroom. The space was half-bedroom, half-office, with a desk and a small filing cabinet located on the left half of the room, and a bed, dresser and closet on the right. Lakin was seated on the bed, peering down at some pieces of paper in his hand.

"Whatcha got there?" I asked, coming to stand in front of him.

"Ticket stubs." Looking up, he handed them to me. "Take a look."

I did, and then frowned. They appeared to be for some kind of betting event, though I couldn't really tell what for. The name

"The Dirty Habit" was scrawled across the backside of the ticket in cramped, messy handwriting.

"The Dirty Habit," I murmured, the name tickling a memory in the back of my mind. "I think that's a bar or nightclub of some kind."

"Is that right?" Lakin stood up so he could look at the tickets over my shoulder. "I don't think there's a club by that name in Solantha, but it must not be too far from here."

"I'll ask Annia about it. She'll probably know."

"Annia?"

"She's an enforcer friend of mine." I winked at the dubious look on his face. "Don't worry, she's one of the good ones."

"Alright, well I trust you." Lakin glanced at his watch. "I should get back to my house soon. I've got a meeting scheduled with one of my deputies."

"Crap," I muttered as I realized it was nearly noon. I had to get back to the Palace!

"Is everything okay?"

"Yeah, yeah, it's fine." But inside I was kicking myself. I hadn't put any time into investigating the bank, or reading the book the Chief Mage had given me last night! "I've just gotta get back to the Palace now. I'll catch you later."

Somehow, I was going to have to figure out how to manage my time better. Otherwise I had a feeling I was going to end up in hot water again.

8

I arrived at the Palace with just enough time to grab a quick lunch before heading down to the Mages Guild. I walked into the large, open lobby that served as the reception and hub of the Guild, but stopped short at the sight of the Chief Mage standing there, talking with Director Chen.

Because the universe hates me sometimes, both of them turned to look at me just as I stuffed the last bite of my sandwich into my mouth. My insides squirmed at the thought of beautiful, perfect Director Chen staring at me while my cheeks were puffed up like a chipmunk's, and I swallowed hastily.

"Miss Baine." Something that looked suspiciously like amusement flickered in Iannis's eyes, but it was gone too quickly for me to call him out on it. "I see that you've managed to be on time for once."

"Yes, well I'm trying to act like a real grown up now."

"I'm glad you made it," Director Chen said smoothly, oblivious to the sarcasm in my voice. "I was actually going to request you join me in my office today, as I am backlogged and could use your assistance. The Secretary of Agricultural Magic tells me you're quite good with paperwork."

Oh for Magorah's sake! The *last* thing I needed was to gain a reputation for being a good admin. The Mages Guild would never give me any other job! I tried to think of something to say that could get me out of this – I wasn't really thrilled about having to spend the afternoon with Director Chen – but I was saved from having to answer as a courier rushed into the room.

"Lord Iannis," he gasped, his round cheeks red with exertion – he was a gangly teenager, around Noria's age. "There's an emergency at the Firegate Bridge!"

"What kind of emergency?" Iannis demanded.

"Some kind of magical attack from the Resistance! They've sent a message saying they're going to destroy the bridge!" the courier held up a sheet of paper.

Ice rippled through me at the mention of the Resistance. Was my cousin Rylan involved? He was a member, and I'd recently heard that the Resistance had been engaging in stunts that had resulted in civilian casualties. I sincerely hoped he wasn't part of such a terrible act.

Iannis snatched the paper from the courier, his violet eyes scanning the words. His mouth tightened. "I will take care of this."

"Sir," Director Chen protested. "You don't need to put yourself at risk –"

"This is my city, and the bridge is an important landmark. I won't leave this up to anyone else."

"I'm coming with you."

The Chief Mage turned toward me, annoyance sparking in his eyes. "You need to stay here –"

"I'm your apprentice," I insisted, standing my ground. I wouldn't outright defy him, not in front of all these people, but I wasn't going to give in on this easily. "I'm supposed to assist you, and this sounds like something you could use help with. Please," I added, softening my tone a little. "Let me come with you."

The 'please' seemed do the trick – some of the annoyance in Iannis's expression lessened. "Fine. But we need to hurry."

"Speed's one thing I'm good at." I winked, then reached for the beast within me. A glowing white light enveloped my body, and I shifted from the form of a young woman to that of a black panther. In the past, I would have had to strip my clothes off to do this, but after seeing Fenris shift back and forth without losing his clothes, I got him to get me a copy of the charm he used so I could do it myself. By the time the glow faded from my vision, Iannis was already gone, likely to fetch a horse. Rather than try to find him, I raced back to the front lobby and out the doors, headed for the bridge myself. I was a lot faster than a horse – jaguars could reach up to sixty-five miles per hour at top speed, and while I couldn't run the whole way to the bridge at that pace, I could still beat Iannis there.

It took me about ten minutes to get to the Firegate Bridge, and to my alarm, it was packed with civilians. Carriages and steamcars rolled forward in their respective lanes, while people strolled along the walkways as if they didn't have a care in the world. By Magorah, but why wasn't anyone warning these people?

"GET OFF THE BRIDGE!" I mentally shouted at the few shifters I saw, knowing that would be more effective than standing here and shouting in human form. *"THE RESISTANCE IS GOING TO DESTROY THE BRIDGE! YOU NEED TO GET OFF!"*

The shifters glanced around in alarm, clearly wondering where the voice was coming from. A few of them turned and saw me, and I repeated the warning. Instantly they turned around and began running for the end of the bridge. Voices rose in alarm, the humans asking what was going on, and one of the shifters repeated my warning. Soon the pedestrians were sprinting en masse towards land, their eyes wide with hysteria, and the vehicles began moving at a faster pace too.

Unfortunately, this resulted in a lot of horn-honking as the steamcars tried to get ahead, and I heard a crunch as a large, grey car smashed into the back of a black one. Meanwhile, pedestrians were trampling over each other in their efforts to clear the bridge.

"Stop knocking each other over!" I shouted, hoping the shifters would listen. But panic had taken over, and nobody seemed to be listening.

The sound of hooves clattering on the sidewalk drew my attention from the crowds, and I turned my head to see the Chief Mage galloping toward me, his long hair and robes streaming out behind him. His eyes were trained on the bridge, and his expression was so fierce I forgot the danger for a moment, struck by how warrior-like he looked.

His eyes shifted toward me, and he drew his horse to a stop. The animal, a beautiful palomino, snorted and pawed the ground, and I put some distance between us before he stomped on my paws.

"I see you've evacuated the Bridge," he said tightly, noting the mass hysteria.

I winced. *"Is there anything you can do about this?"* I didn't know how to get these people to behave.

"Yes," Iannis said. He pressed a hand to his throat and muttered a Word, then shouted, *"Fai'grynal!"*

A wave of magic swept across the bridge, and everybody froze. Literally. The people stopped mid-run, and the cars all rolled to a halt. My ears rang from the force of Iannis's shout – he'd magically amplified his voice so that everyone could hear him.

"Ladies and gentlemen," he called, "I know you are all frightened, but you need to exit the bridge in an orderly fashion!"

Many of the shifters and humans glared at him, but since they were frozen there was little else they could do. "I'm going to unfreeze you now, and you are all going to move to the exit at a brisk, but controlled pace. Anyone out of line will be frozen again, and left stuck on the bridge."

Well that's one way to do it, I thought as I watched eyes widen with panic. Iannis spoke another word, unfreezing the citizens. Many of them fell over, but they quickly dusted themselves off and began moving forward.

"Thanks," I said, relief coursing through me as I saw that the civilians were no longer trying to kill each other in their haste to escape. I filed away the Words Iannis used, in case I had to stop a mass riot or something in the future. Unlikely, but with the way my life was going you never knew.

"Did the message from the Resistance say when this attack was supposed to take place?"

"No." Iannis scowled. "They were not quite that helpful." His gaze turned back toward the bridge. "I can tell that magic was used here recently – the protective wards that are normally active around the bridge have been deactivated. I'll need to cast a spell to determine what was else was done."

"No need," I told him, lifting my nose to scent the air. I peeled back my upper lip so I could make full use of the scent gland hidden beneath there – my olfactory senses were ten times stronger as a panther. *"I can already tell where the source is coming from."*

Without waiting for an answer, I raced up the walkway, following the strange scent that I'd caught from the moment I'd arrived at the bridge – a combination of magic and sulfur. The scent grew stronger as I approached the first of the two red towers from which the bridge was suspended, and my senses told me that whatever the spell was, it had been cast here.

"What is it?" the Chief Mage demanded, having followed me on his horse. "Did you find something?"

"I think it's under the bridge."

"Mac soith!" Iannis swore, and I blinked at the unfamiliar language, guessing it was his homeland tongue. From what I understood, Iannis was originally from Manuc, an island country on the opposite side of the sea from the East Coast. A faint whisper of a musical accent was always in his voice, but I'd never heard him speak anything other than English and Loranian before now.

"Don't worry. I can get under there." Nervous energy crackled through me at the idea of getting so close to the bomb, but I had no idea how much time was left before the thing went off. We couldn't afford to wait for someone else to get here – I was going to have to take the risk.

I slid my body beneath the railing of the fence, then shimmied onto one of the beams that crisscrossed along the side of the bridge. Fear rippled through me at the sight of bundles of traxtoline fastened all across the underside of the bridge – enough to blow a huge hole that would collapse the structure, especially with the weight of cars and carriages atop it. Near the side of the bridge that I was on, a kind of device was wired to the sticks of traxtoline, and there was a timer fastened to that, ticking down, down, down. The device itself was mechanical – the magic was coming from some kind of glowing substance that fastened the traxtoline to the underside of the bridge, something that I instinctively knew would make it impossible for me to remove both the traxtoline and the device.

"Iannis," I said, my mental voice trembling a little. *"There's a really big bomb down here. And I think it's about to go off* really *soon."*

If the Chief Mage had any problem with me using his given

name, he chose not to voice it now. "You need to freeze it," he shouted from above. "That's the only way to stop it."

"In shifter form?" I demanded. I'd never tried to use magic in beast form before, and while I figured it should theoretically be possible, I wasn't confident about it. I didn't know the Words necessary to conjure enough ice to freeze both the device and the traxtoline. In this form the beast half of me tended to come more to the forefront, and it was afraid of magic. I was worried that I might lose control.

"I'll help you," Iannis called, and then he murmured something, something too quiet for me to hear. In the next second I gasped at a strange presence within me – the presence of another soul.

"Relax," Iannis's voice echoed in my mind, and I froze as I realized that somehow, he'd managed to get *inside* me. This was much more invasive than mind-speech, not only could I feel his concern and urgency, but I could actually feel Iannis's essence inside me, a strange combination of icy-hot that made me shiver. *"Let me guide you."*

Closing my eyes, I drew in a deep breath, then forced my muscles to relax. Iannis told me the Words of the spell, and then a hot, electric current began flowing through me – his own magic, melding with mine. The only time something similar had happened was when he'd unlocked my powers, and it was a sensation I doubted I would ever get used to.

I opened my eyes and focused in on the explosive, more confident now. Even though an onlooker would simply see a lone panther clinging to the side of the bridge, Iannis was with me, almost as if he stood right behind me, guiding me with his own hands. I unwrapped one of my limbs from the beam and stretched the pad of my front paw toward the device, and then I spoke the Words in my mind, directing my intent through them.

Frigid magic spilled out of my paw, sending ice crackling

across the device. The timer jumped, and my heart stopped for a moment, paralyzed at the idea that I might have accidentally set off the device before the bundles of traxtoline had frozen. But the device didn't go off, and the magic quickly spread, running across the length of explosives until they were completely encased in ice. The magic continued back and forth a couple of times, covering the bomb with layer upon layer of ice, and I didn't stop until the timer had ceased to move from within the frozen block.

"Excellent job," Iannis said. "Now we need to get rid of it."

"Okay." I eyed the explosives nervously. "How are we going to do that?"

There was silence for a moment. "I believe the easiest way would be to use an alchemical spell to turn the device itself into ice."

"Wait, what? You can actually do that?"

"Yes." Dry humor tinged Iannis's voice. "Alchemical magic is a little beyond your scope, so I'll have to work directly through you this time. Hold out your paw, as before."

I did as he asked, and listened as Iannis spoke another incantation in my mind. The spell activated, and I goggled at the amount of energy that came pouring out of my paws – if Iannis hadn't been lending me his magic I would certainly have used all mine up, and probably fallen into the bay from exhaustion. I watched as the magic penetrated through the layers of ice and seeped into the explosive device like water soaking into a sponge. It took several minutes, but gradually the device turned more and more translucent, until it was barely distinguishable from the block of ice encasing it.

"Excellent," Iannis said when it was done. "Now come back up."

He withdrew from me then, and the sudden change was so shocking I nearly lost my grip on the beam and went tumbling into the water -- a fall that could potentially kill me. Trembling, I clung to the beam for a long moment until I felt sure of myself, then slowly pulled myself back up to the surface.

"Are you hurt?" Iannis demanded the moment I was topside. He jumped from his horse to crouch down in front of me, meeting my eyes.

"I'm fine. Just a little shaky. Give me a minute."

The majority of the bridge was empty now, save for a few abandoned carriages and steamcars. Still, I was surprised when Iannis sat down on the curb next to me and stroked a hand down my fur. A warm current flowed down my spine, banishing some of the hollow, icy feeling, and I had to resist the urge to lean into him. His masculine scent was incredibly compelling, and as he sat beside me on the bridge, looking at me with such concern in his eyes, he was more approachable than he'd ever been.

But I didn't lean on him, because that would break the barrier that had mutually been erected between us, and there was no coming back from that.

Once my heartbeat had steadied, I pushed myself to my feet, then shifted back into human form. By the time my vision had cleared, Iannis was standing, his expression stern once again. But there was a look in his eye I'd never seen before, something that could almost be mistaken for admiration.

"Perhaps I could have found a way to do this without you, but I probably would not have found the explosive device in time. Thank you for insisting on coming along."

I grinned at that. "That's the first time you've ever thanked me for my stubbornness."

"Indeed." He hesitated, uncertainty flickering in his eyes for a moment. "The magic I used to help you defuse the bomb... I would appreciate it if you kept it to yourself. It is not something I'd care to share with others."

"Umm, okay." My brows furrowed in confusion. "What, did

you use black magic or something?" What he'd done hadn't felt evil, but it had certainly thrown me off. If Iannis could do something as crazy as invade my *soul*, what else was he capable of?

"Not black magic, just… unconventional." He frowned. "I would rather not explain myself further."

"Fine." I held up a hand – it really wasn't that important, and I didn't want to strain our relationship after things seemed to finally be moving in a better direction. "I won't ask questions. Your secret is safe with me."

"Thank you." He gave me another small smile. "As a reward for your good work today, I'm giving you the rest of the day off."

"You what?"

"You heard me," he said dryly as he swung himself up onto his horse. "Try not to waste it. You'll be back to work in the Guild tomorrow afternoon."

My grin widened as he galloped away, and I was so happy that it didn't even occur to me until he was out of sight that I didn't have a ride back to the Palace.

9

*A*fter allowing myself a few more minutes of rest, I shifted back into beast form and trotted back to the Palace. From there I grabbed my steambike and rode to the Enforcer's Guild to see if Annia was there.

Sure enough, she was sitting at her desk, cursing under her breath as she filled out what looked like a mountain of paperwork. With her pale skin, long auburn hair and dark eyes, she was a more sophisticated version of her younger sister Noria, without the freckles or the frizz. Her slender but fully formed curves were covered from head to toe in black denim, and I arched a brow as I sat down in the seat next to her desk.

"Dressing casual today?" I asked. Enforcers usually wore leather while we were on the job – it was sturdier than any cloth, which was important in our line of work.

Annia jerked her head up at the sound of my voice. "Oh hey. Nice to see you too."

I grinned at her peeved tone. "You didn't answer my question."

"Yes," she said, returning her attention to the paper she was scribbling away at – she was filling out the forms required to claim her fee on a bounty she'd turned in. "After I fill out this flaming pile of paperwork, I'm taking the day off. So don't even think about asking me for work, because that is a four-letter word today."

"I think it's a four-letter word every day," I teased, earning myself a dirty look. I didn't take any offense though – Annia hated paperwork with a fiery passion, and sitting down to fill out the stuff always put her in a foul temper. "I'm actually not here looking for work. I was wondering if you might be able to answer a question I've got about a case."

"You've got a case?" Annia's eyebrows arched as she straightened in her seat, curiosity gleaming in her dark eyes. "I haven't seen you around here in forever. When did you have time to grab a case?"

"Well, it's not an Enforcer's Guild case," I admitted. "It's something that Inspector Lakin is working on, and I've agreed to help him with it."

"Really? He's paying you for it?"

"I wish." My mouth twisted into a grimace. "No, actually I'm doing this one pro-bono. It's connected to the silver murders, and more specifically, Sillara's death."

"Oh." Annia set her pen down – she'd liked Sillara too. "Well that's a whole different story, then. What can I do to help?"

I pulled out the betting tickets and handed them to Annia. "Lakin and I found these at the house of a reporter who went missing recently. They've got the name of a business on the back of it, and I was hoping you might know what and where it is, because it sounds familiar to me."

"The Dirty Habit?" Annia asked, her brown eyes sparking with recognition. "Sure, that's a gambling den in Turain. Legal stuff, usually cards and pool. I've been there once or twice."

"Right." That explained why I'd never been there. I stayed away from gambling joints – I was bad enough at managing money as it was, and didn't need another reason to spend it. Turain was further up the coast, outside Solantha County but definitely still part of the State of Canalo. "You a regular over there?"

"Not really." Annia handed the slips back to me, then picked up her pen and turned her eyes back towards the stack of forms in front of her. "I've only been there once, about two years ago when I was running down a lead."

"Well, I've recently gained a reputation for being good at paperwork at the Mages Guild," I said wryly. "What do you say I use my newfound skill to help you out, and then you come with me to Turain to check out this gambling den and see if something doesn't pop?"

"Hmm." Annia dragged her front teeth over her bottom lip as she considered. "That sounds a lot like work."

"Aww, c'mon Annia." I nudged her shoulder. "For Sillara, right?"

"Okay. But only if you can help me get this done in the next hour. I still fully intend to enjoy some downtime today, so if I'm here longer than that I'm not going."

I grimaced as I reached for the stack of papers next to Annia's elbow and drew them toward me. "Well, I always do like a challenge."

WE FINISHED with time to spare, and rode across the bridge and up the coast to Turain – a little over an hour's ride on my bike. The gambling den was located in Turain's Maintown, so I used a magical illusion to disguise myself as a petite blonde human with hazel eyes and a beach tan, exchanging my leathers for a short silver dress and black, knee high boots.

Annia, still dressed in the same black denim she'd worn to

the Guild, rolled her eyes at my clubby getup. "You planning on taking someone home tonight?" she asked, arching a dark red brow.

"No." I batted my eyelashes and looped an arm around her waist, clinging close. "But we're a lesbian couple now, and I have to look the part. You're the stud, and I'm the femme."

Annia snorted. "Would have been nice if you'd filled me in on the plan before we got here. Are you going by a different name, then?"

"Nadia." The name popped from my lips, and it took me a moment to remember that it was the name the Chief Mage had given me when we'd gone similarly undercover at a bar in Solantha's Maintown. Warmth spread through me as I remembered how casual he'd been, looping his arms around my waist and sitting me down in his lap as if I'd actually been his girlfriend. He'd glamoured himself up to look like a young human college student, and he'd played the part so well it had been a little disconcerting.

"Alright Nadia." Annia's lips twitched with laughter as I squeezed her arm, and she tugged me a little closer to her body, playing the part. "Let's do this."

We walked into the club, a black-painted cinder block building on the corner of the street, and were assailed by a haze of cigarette smoke. Instantly, I broke into a coughing fit, and held up my hand, my eyes watering. I *hated* cigarettes with a passion – I was ridiculously sensitive to the smoke and it always had this effect on me.

"Get it together," Annia hissed in my ear. "People are staring." Sure enough, a few of the patrons seated around the various round tables set up throughout the space were turning to look at me, their eyebrows raised as if to say 'What? You've never been around smoke before?' I wanted to bare my teeth at them and tell them to fuck off, but that didn't go with the sweet, girlish persona I was affecting, so instead I turned and buried my nose in Annia's jacket to try and regain my composure.

"Nice," she muttered, but she stroked a hand across my back comfortingly.

"Can I get you ladies anything?" The bartender asked. "Maybe some water for your girl?" He gazed pointedly at me.

"Oh yeah, that'd be great." Annia tugged me over to the bar, and I forced myself to pull my face away from her jacket and sit down on one of the stools. Fortunately, the smoke happened to be coming from a group sitting in a corner at the opposite end of the room, and the smell was less pungent here. "Can you get a glass of water for her, and a scotch for me? I could do with something strong to get me started."

"Coming right up." The bartender smiled at Annia, then served up our drinks. I forced myself to sip my water slowly instead of gulping it down – being ladylike really wasn't my thing. Why did I decide to do this again?

Oh, right. For the victims.

"Not really sure what I'm supposed to do now," I muttered to Annia, feeling a little put out. "I'm going to have a tough time blending in around here enough to ask questions." I should have thought this through a little better.

Annia grinned at me over her half empty glass. "Don't you worry your pretty little head about it, sweetheart," she said, putting an arm around my shoulder and planting a kiss on my cheek. "You just sit next to me and look gorgeous, and I'll do all the talking."

I scratched the side of my head with my middle finger, and Annia nearly choked on her drink. We finished up at the bar, and then she led me over to one of the card tables. I eyed the heavy money pouch at her hip enviously as she withdrew a handful of coins to buy chips from the dealer – Annia had really been cashing in on the bounties lately.

As Annia suggested, I sat next to her and looked pretty while she played with the big boys, going through several rounds of Mad Jack at this table, and then moving on to another one to play Seven Card. I simply batted my eyelashes at the men, cooing and praising Annia every time she won a round – which was quite often, to my surprise. Annia might not've been a regular around here, but she was definitely no stranger to playing cards. Between her good looks and her natural gift of gab, she got the men to relax and chat with her despite the fact that she was taking their money.

"So," Annia finally said to the man next to her after they closed out another round. "My brother gave me some betting tickets awhile back that I never ended up using, and I forgot what they were for. Think you might be able to help me out? I'm looking to find something new to spend my money on."

"Sure." The man took the tickets from Annia, but the smile from his face faded as he stared down at the tickets. "You said your brother gave these to you?"

"Yeah." Annia arched a brow. "There a problem with that?"

"Well, no..." The man's forehead furrowed, as if he wasn't quite sure how to explain. "I mean, it's just that this isn't the type of betting ring you usually buy tickets as gifts for, at least not for a woman."

"In case you haven't noticed, I'm not the average woman," Annia drawled, looping an arm around my shoulders and drawing me close. I smiled vapidly and pressed a hand to her chest, and the other man grinned.

"No, that you're not," he agreed. "I can tell you're a woman who can handle herself, so I guess you'd enjoy this kind of thing." He glanced around the room, then lowered his voice. "These betting tickets are for the Shifter Royale."

"The Shifter Royale?" Annia echoed. "What's that?"

"It's an underground fight club where different types of

shifters are pitted against each other," the man murmured. "I've only been to a fight once myself, and I have to say it's pretty brutal. Definitely not for the faint of heart."

I stiffened at that, and Annia gave my shoulder a warning squeeze. "Well that sounds exciting. Where do I get seats?"

"Silon can help you out with that." The man nodded toward the back corner of the room, and I stifled a groan, knowing he was referring to the table of smokers. *Figures.* "He's the one who sells the admission tickets. There are bookies at the event itself to take your bets, of course."

"Good to know." Annia turned her head in my direction and gave me another squeeze. "Hey Nadia, I'm gonna go over there and talk to Silon. Why don't you hang out at the bar for a second? I'll be right back."

"Sure thing sweetheart," I purred as she kissed me on the cheek, relieved that Annia was giving me an out. Much as I would have liked to go with her, I would be useless standing next to her just hacking and coughing, and my shifter hearing would allow me to overhear the conversation anyway.

"Buy three tickets," I murmured in her ear as I stood up, and then I went to sit at the bar again as she'd told me to. I watched out of the corner of my eye as Annia approached Silon, a stocky, bald guy with a bushy red beard and a cigar shoved between the corners of his lips. He didn't look too friendly as Annia approached, and when one of the men at the table stood up to frisk Annia for recording devices or any other suspicious items, I was glad that she'd left her enforcer bracelet at home. Once that was out of the way, Silon relaxed and sold her the tickets without further fuss. He told her that the show was for tomorrow night, then gave her an address. It was all pretty straightforward, almost ridiculously so.

"Well tomorrow night should be interesting," Annia commented once we were outside the club.

"No kidding," I spat as we rounded the block, heading for my bike. "Underground shifter fights? There's no way in hell that's legal."

"I doubt the shifters are being hurt too badly," Annia said, but her voice was heavy with disapproval. "I mean, whoever's running this thing is clearly making money off the fights, so they'll want to keep the shifters alive for repeat performances."

"By Magorah," I hissed, outrage sizzling in my gut. "I can't believe there are humans using shifters for sport! It's slavery all over again, except this time it's not the mages who are responsible."

"You don't know that," Annia said darkly as she settled herself behind me on the bike. "There are rogue mages out there who consider themselves above the law, and one could be pulling the strings here."

"Well regardless if they're human or mage, they're going to pay," I growled, tightening my grip around the handlebars. I kicked off with a shrill whistle from my engine, and left Turain behind in a cloud of steam. I would be back tomorrow, and when I did I was going to blow a hole in this scheme and find out what was really going on. I was going to drag the cruel son of a bitch behind this out of his hidey-hole.

10

I dropped Annia off at her apartment in Maintown, then passed by Lakin's house on the way home to tell him about the underground ring and that we had tickets for tomorrow night. He wasn't home, so I picked the lock on the front door and left a note for him on his refrigerator with the details and my phone number – I wasn't about to leave sensitive information like that on his doorstep.

I considered going to the Palace and telling the Chief Mage about what I'd found, but he had a lot on his mind and I didn't want to burden him when I didn't actually need his help yet. I would tell him when the time was right, probably after I went to the fighting ring myself tomorrow. So instead I headed home to resume my study of the *Residah*.

The phone started ringing almost as soon as I walked into my apartment, and I scowled. Not a single phone call in weeks, and now I was getting two in as many days?

You left Lakin your phone number, remember? He's probably just calling you back.

Oh! Right. My mood lifted, and I quickly crossed the room to snatch up the phone.

"Hey! Thanks for calling me back."

"I wasn't aware you'd tried to contact me." I nearly dropped the phone at the dry sound of my cousin Rylan's voice. "Maybe you sent me a note to explain why you recklessly endangered yourself on the Firegate Bridge today?"

"You have *got* to be kidding me," I exploded, the initial pleasure at hearing the sound of my cousin's voice evaporating as he reminded me of the terrorist attack Iannis and I had thwarted. "You're scolding me for saving hundreds of people today after *you* put them all in danger just to make a political statement? How fucking dare you!"

"I didn't organize the attack on the bridge!" Rylan protested sharply. "If I had, I would have made sure to keep civilians out of harm's way. Believe it or not, I don't actually have a hand in *everything* the Resistance does."

"Maybe not, but you knew about it, didn't you?" I charged bitterly. "You could have sent out a warning or something, instead of keeping me in the dark about a potential mass murder."

"I'm a soldier in this army, Naya," Rylan said defensively. "It's my job to follow orders, not make up my own. And you're making my job really difficult by throwing yourself in harm's way.

"Oh, well I'm so sorry about that," I spat. "I'll be more considerate the next time I have to evacuate several hundred civilians from a bridge that's about to explode."

"Naya –"

"Save it," I snapped. "I don't need to hear another lecture about your noble and glorious cause. How about you tell me something useful for once? Have you found out anything about the Benefactor like I asked you to?"

"I've had bigger things to worry about recently," Rylan snapped back, "and so do you, Naya."

"Why?" I demanded. "What aren't you telling me?"

"All I'm going to say is that you need to watch your back. You're painting a big target on it every time you interfere with the Resistance's plans."

"Gee, thanks. I'll make sure to grow a second pair of eyes out of the back of my head."

"Are you planning on accompanying the Chief Mage to the Convention this year?" Rylan asked, ignoring my sarcasm.

"No." I blinked at the change of subject. "Why?'

"I highly suggest you don't, if you value your life."

"And just what is that supposed to mean?"

"Exactly what it sounds like. And trust me Naya, if you warn the Chief Mage about this, the Resistance will definitely consider you an enemy of the people and treat you accordingly."

"This is unbelievable! Rylan, just tell me what's going on –"

"Goodbye, little cousin. I hope you make the right choice."

The phone went dead, and I had a feeling Rylan wouldn't be calling me again. By Magorah, but what had happened to him? Of all my family, he was the only one I'd been truly close with, mainly because we both shared a rebellious streak. But the Rylan who'd run off to join the Resistance had still believed in the idea of true justice, and would never have put his support behind an organization that condoned terrorist attacks and senseless destruction. Bombing the Firegate Bridge was both, and I just couldn't understand how Rylan could possibly be okay with killing all those people.

I set the receiver back down in its cradle, then stared at it, wondering if I should call the Palace to warn the Chief Mage, or tell him in person. There was no way I could leave Iannis in the dark about something like this. On the one hand, Rylan's warning had been vague – he could have simply meant that if I came along and interfered in whatever the Resistance had planned that they would kill me. But now that I knew what the

Resistance was capable of, the Chief Mage's life might be in some kind of danger.

It's probably better not to call, I thought. I didn't know if the Resistance had a way of monitoring my phone calls, but considering their resources were growing, I couldn't discount the possibility. No, it was better for me to go in person.

But just as I was reaching for my jacket, someone started pounding at my door.

"Sunaya!" A familiar voice shrieked, and I froze – it was my cousin Melantha, Mafiela's oldest and most favored child. "Sunaya Baine, open this door right now!"

Annoyed and alarmed all at once, I strode over to the door and glared through the peephole. Sure enough, Melantha stood there, dressed in a dark blouse and a pair of jeans, her blonde hair perfectly curled around the diamond-shaped face that was so very much like her mother's. And like her mother, we hated each other passionately, something that distance and time clearly hadn't lessened, as her yellow eyes were burning with rage.

"What the fuck do you want?" I snarled as I yanked the door open.

"You bitch!" Melantha shrieked, launching herself at me with her claws outstretched. I was so surprised that I didn't move out of the way fast enough, and she knocked me to the ground. I yowled as her claws raked across my face, leaving a burning trail of fire and blood. "You're going to pay for this!"

"What are you talking about?" I shouted, raising my arms to block the blows. Blood streamed down my forearms as she shredded my skin with her claws, and I hissed at the pain from the deep gashes. Pissed, I bucked my hips hard and twisted my body, flipping us over and pinning her to the ground. "Pay for *what*?"

"My daughter is gone!" Melantha howled, tears streaming

from her blazing eyes. "They've taken Mika, and it's all your fault!"

"What?" I recoiled, completely dumbstruck. That couldn't be right. The mysterious man, whoever he was, had only called yesterday. They couldn't have followed through on their threat so soon!

"She's been gone since this afternoon, and I know it's your fault!" Melantha snarled, and then she kicked me in the chest, sending me flying back several feet. One of my ribs crunched, and I cried out in pain.

"Are you fucking kidding me?" I growled, struggling to my feet. Normally Melantha wouldn't have been able to wipe the floor with me like this, but her announcement about Mika had shocked the shit out of me, giving her the upper hand. "She hasn't been gone for twenty-four hours yet and you're already calling her missing? How do you know she didn't just go out with some friends?"

"Because she told me she was going out to the backyard to work on her homework, and the next thing I knew she was gone!" Melantha jumped to her feet, claws extended as she bared her fangs at me. "Mother told me that you came to our house with a warning this morning. I should have known you were too selfish to do as the man asked and stop meddling in whatever mess you've gotten yourself into!" She rushed me again.

"THAT'S ENOUGH!" I shouted, flinging an arm out. Blue-green flames ignited around my fist, and Melantha skidded to a halt, fear flashing in her yellow eyes. She hissed at the sight of the flame in my hand, but shrank back – like all shifters, she was afraid of magic, and unlike me she didn't have mage blood running through her veins to help counteract the instinct to run away.

"You're an abomination," she spat at me. "Your life should have been terminated while you were still in the womb!"

"Shut the fuck up before I burn you to a crisp," I snapped, my body trembling with rage and pain. "I'm sorry about your daughter, Melantha, and I'll do my best to find her. But if you don't get out of my apartment right now, I'm going to kill you."

"May Magorah curse you and all your progeny!" she snarled, and then slammed the door behind her as she left.

I shook my head as I slumped to the ground. With the way my life was going right now, I wasn't going to have any progeny to curse.

I SHIFTED into beast form to heal my wounds, then tried to get some shuteye, but I was too distressed to sleep. So instead, I left my apartment, still in panther form, and trotted down to Lakin's house in Shiftertown. I was too hungry and tired to shift back, but I needed to know what he was doing to find my cousin's daughter.

By the time I reached Lakin's house, my tail was dragging from exhaustion, but I managed to reach up on my hind legs and press the doorbell with my paw. I dropped back down onto all fours, then sat on his front step as I wearily waited for him to answer.

"Who is it?" he called through the door, sounding tired. "This isn't exactly the best time."

"*It's me*," I said, using mindspeech to communicate. "*Please, Boon, let me in.*"

"Naya?" There was a click, and then Lakin opened the door, shock on his lean face that quickly melted into sympathy. "Are you here about Mika?"

"*Yes,*" I said, and he stepped aside so I could come in. "*Melantha just came by my house for a visit.*"

"Shit," Lakin muttered as he shut the door behind me. "I hope she didn't trash your apartment. I know all about how crazy mothers can get when their young are in danger."

"*The apartment's fine, thanks.*" I hopped up onto the stuffed green couch – a new addition – and curled up, resting my chin on top of my paws.

Lakin paused at the annoyance in my words. "I didn't mean to imply I wasn't concerned for your own well-being," he said gently, coming to sit next to me on the couch. He stroked a hand hesitantly over my fur, reminding me of how Iannis had done the same back on the bridge. "You seem exhausted. I'm guessing you had to heal yourself?"

"*Yeah,*" I admitted with a little sigh. "*And I already hadn't eaten. Guess it's going to take me awhile to recharge.*"

"Let me get you some food," Lakin said, standing up. "You need the fuel."

My stomach twisted at the idea of eating, but I knew I wasn't in any position to turn down food. My fridge was empty, and I wasn't going to make it to the Palace tonight to raid their kitchens. Eating while I was already there was one thing, but I'd never live it down if Iannis discovered I was making trips to the Palace just for a meal.

Lakin came back with a huge stainless steel bowl filled with steaks, and my stomach growled at the scent of raw meat. My beast half took over, pouncing on the bowl as Lakin set it down on the ground, and I ripped into the meat with savage intensity. Lakin said nothing, simply sat on the couch and watched as I devoured the steaks, and I kept my own gaze focused on my food, not wanting to see the pity in his eyes.

"Feeling better?" he asked after I'd finished and laid myself down on the floor.

"Yes." Not completely of course – my heart was still a roiling mass of emotion – but the weight of food in my belly helped calm me a little. I raised my eyes to Lakin's. *"Thank you. I'm sorry for intruding like this."*

"It's not a problem," Lakin said gently. "You've had a rough day."

He didn't know how rough. And I wasn't going to tell him – the phone call from Rylan wasn't really Lakin's business, and there was nothing Lakin could do about it anyway. I was just going to have to tell Iannis when I saw him next, and as Rylan said, watch my back.

"So have you found anything?" I asked. *"Any clue as to who might've taken Mika?"*

"The only clue is that phone call you received yesterday," Lakin said, his lips thinning. "I canvassed the neighborhood, but nobody saw who took Mika. The only lead we have right now is that fighting ring you've dug up."

"Got it. You're coming with us to the Shifter Royale tomorrow, right?"

"Of course. I wouldn't miss out on the chance to investigate such an important lead."

I got to my feet, then turned my mind inward and reached for the human half of me so I could shift back. I had enough food in my belly, but mentally I was so exhausted that by the time I finished I collapsed onto the couch next to Lakin.

"Do you need a place to crash?" Lakin asked, studying me with concern. "Sometimes it can be tough to be alone in situations like this."

"Thanks, but it's not necessary." I shook my head, smiling a little. "I've been alone long enough that I've figured out how to deal."

"Just because you've figured out how to be alone doesn't mean you have to be," Lakin said softly. He cupped my cheek with his hand, and my heart started beating faster at the tender look in his eyes.

"Lakin –"

"My name is Boon," he murmured, and then he closed the distance between us. I drew a sharp breath in through my nostrils as he kissed me, softly, slowly, his lips a gentle caress against mine. Warmth stole through me, softening me up, and I closed my eyes, leaning into him. Cupping my face with both hands, he deepened the kiss, sliding his tongue in my mouth. He tasted dark and smoky, like a hot fire on a cold night, and he warmed me from the inside out.

"I can smell your need," he murmured against my mouth, hot gaze boring deeply into mine. "I know you're going to need a male soon."

"Yes." I licked my lips, tasting the desire on my own tongue. It slowly built with each passing day as my heat approached, and though I still had a few weeks until that day came, that didn't necessarily mean my body wanted to be celibate in the meantime. But as I stared into Lakin's reddish-yellow eyes, a pair of iridescent violet irises flashed in my mind's eye, and heat for a different individual rushed through me.

"Boon," I said as Lakin leaned into me. "I'm not sure I'm ready for this." I was being stupid, I knew – Lakin was an obvious choice, both as a lover and a potential mate, and I already knew I could never have Iannis. But I was conflicted all the same, and I wasn't going to get involved with someone I worked with while my heart was still tangled up.

"Alright." Lakin drew back, disappointment in his gaze, but he gave me a small smile all the same. "I won't push you. Just know that I'm here."

"I do know." I squeezed his hand, then stood up. "I'd better get back home."

"Are you sure?" Lakin asked, rising to his feet as well. "I've got a couch now, you know." He gave me a crooked grin, and I knew he was also telling me without words that his bed was available too.

"Yeah, I'm sure." I gave him a grin of my own. "But my bed gets lonely when I'm not in it. You'll be at the Enforcer's Guild at six o'clock tomorrow afternoon?"

"That's the plan." His gaze darkened. "It's going to be tough to just stand there at the Royale and observe."

"Tell me about it." I bit my lip as I left, turning the idea over in my mind. Reconnaissance was not my strong suit, not when innocent people were being hurt, but if I was going to get to the mastermind behind this I was going to have to hold back. I just hoped I could keep my mouth shut long enough to get through the Royale, or we were all going to be in deep trouble.

11

By the time I made it back to my apartment, exhaustion had caught up with me, and I fell asleep as soon as my head hit the pillow. Dreams came to me that night, or rather faces – my mother, sad but smiling, Roanas, stern but encouraging, and Melantha, furious and despondent all at once. There were other faces too – their features in shadow but for their colorful shifter eyes, luminous with pain and desperation. I knew instinctively that these were the faces of the missing, and that all of them were trying to tell me the same thing – I needed to find out where they were and bring them home.

When I woke up, the grief and fury in my heart was gone, replaced with a single-minded determination. I was going to find out who did this, and when I did I would bring them in, dead or alive. True, my relationship with the Jaguar Clan was strained, but they were still my mother's people, and they didn't deserve this. No one did.

I was just coming out of the shower, a towel wrapped around my body, when my phone rang once again. Resigned to the fact that my apartment was no longer a place of solitude, I walked into the kitchen and answered it, fully expecting another threatening phone call.

"What is it now?"

"Good morning, Miss Baine." I blinked at the sound of Dira's cool voice – the same secretary who'd called when I was at Comenius's shop. "I'm calling on behalf of the Chief Mage. He requests your presence in his study at nine o'clock this morning."

"What?" A quick glance at the clock on my wall had me scowling – it was already eight-thirty! "But I had the morning off!"

"I'm afraid I'm just the messenger, Miss Baine," Dira said lightly, not at all bothered by the fact that she was throwing off my plans for the morning. "I suggest you leave soon if you want to make it on time."

"Thanks," I muttered, hanging up the phone. *Oh well*, I thought as I rushed back into my bedroom to pull on some clothing. I needed to warn Iannis about the threat from the Resistance sooner rather than later anyway. I might as well fit that in around whatever else he wanted to see me about this morning.

The weather was hotter than usual today, so I chose a bright red clingy tank top to wear with my leather pants and jacket. Even the breeze rushing past me as I rode my steambike up to the Mage's Quarter wasn't enough to cool me, and by the time I arrived at Solantha Palace I was hot enough that I slipped off my jacket and carried it over one shoulder. The usual stares followed me as I strode through the halls toward the Chief Mage's study, but I noticed they lingered less than usual. Maybe the Palace residents were actually getting used to my presence.

As I approached the door, the sound of several voices talking made me pause. Was I not the only one being summoned today?

Maybe Dira had been wrong about the time, and Iannis wasn't actually ready to see me yet.

"Hello?" I called, knocking on the door. "It's Sunaya."

The voices on the other side quieted. "Come in, Miss Baine," the Chief Mage called back.

I opened the door, then froze as I took in the number of people in the room. No, it was clear that I wasn't the only one who'd been summoned. Fenris stood at Iannis's side, as usual, and Director Chen was there too... but to my surprise Inspector Lakin was also there, and next to him a gangly teenager with pale brown hair dressed in a set of red mage's robes.

"Morning, Naya," Inspector Lakin said with a grin.

"Morning," I said, my eyebrows raised. "Didn't realize I was being invited to a party."

"I believe the term 'meeting' would be more accurate," the Chief Mage said mildly, drawing the attention of the room back toward him. "We all know each other, correct?"

"I think so," I said slowly, turning toward the young mage. "You're Elnos Ragga, right? Noria's boyfriend?"

"At your service." He gave me a crooked grin as he bowed, and I grinned a little as his gangly body tried to execute the motion. He was a strange combination of charming and awkward, and I could already see why Noria liked him.

"Same to you." I bowed back, then turned back toward the Chief Mage. "So what's this all about?"

"These three are here to make a report, and I wanted you to be here for it," Iannis said, gesturing toward Director Chen, Elnos and Lakin. "I'd prefer you come stand on this side of the desk, if you wouldn't mind."

"Oh. Right." Slightly flustered, I moved around the desk to come stand next to Iannis, on the opposite side of where Fenris stood. Fenris gave me a quick wink as I did, relaxing me a little – it made sense that I would stand next to the Chief Mage as his apprentice, but I was far more used to being on the other side of the desk.

"Very well," the Chief Mage said, settling his violet gaze on Director Chen. "Deliver your report."

"Yes, sir." Director Chen's silk robes rustled lightly around her as she stepped forward – she'd chosen to wear robin's egg blue today, with silver leaves embroidered across the fabric with fine thread. "As some of you may you already know, Inspector Lakin came to the Mages Guild two weeks ago with evidence that shifter-specific drugs are still being sold on the market."

"He did?" I blurted out before I could stop myself.

Annoyance at the interruption briefly disturbed Director Chen's placid expression, but she nodded. "Yes. He confiscated a bag of *incidium* from a wolf shifter. Apparently the shifter bought the supply from a human downtown, and was planning on reselling it to friends and family." Her lip curled ever so slightly.

"By Magorah," I muttered, disgust curling in my own gut. It was bad enough that humans were peddling the stuff around, but for shifters to be selling it to their own kind now? *Incidium* was a fine white powder that created an intense euphoria when ingested, and like all other drugs, shifters were normally impervious to it. But thanks to Elnos, we found out that the drugs were being mixed with silver, which was being masked by kalois, the same plant used in the silver poisonings. Since shifters are highly allergic to silver, the substance counteracts our high metabolisms, allowing the drugs to take effect. Once we'd discovered this, the Enforcer's Guild had started taking a hard stance against drug dealers, and we'd managed to get most of it off the market... or so we'd thought.

"Unless we eradicate the source of these drugs they will continue to be a problem," Elnos, who seemed to be reading my mind, commented. "And according to Inspector Lakin, there have been more episodes of psychotic breaks in Shiftertown."

"Is this true?" Fenris demanded, folding his arms over his broad chest. His yellow eyes narrowed, and I resisted the urge to arch a brow as he sized up Lakin. At times Fenris seemed to act more like the mages he lived with than the shifter he clearly was, but his territorial instincts were showing up loud and clear now.

"Not as many as there were when the drug dealing was rampant, but we had an incident just last week with a rabbit shifter," Lakin said calmly. He met Fenris's eyes, then lowered them ever so slightly – a submission he likely wouldn't have granted if they'd been in Shiftertown instead of the Palace. "The Rabbit Clan ended up having to put him down."

I winced at that. Rabbit shifters weren't known for their ferocity, or for any sort of violence at all, really. They'd been bred as couriers and spies, not as warriors, and the idea of executing one of their own would be abhorrent to them.

"So, do we have any leads that might get us to the manufacturer?" I demanded. "This can't continue."

"The only lead we had was Petros Yantz, and as he is currently in the wind that is not much help to us," Director Chen admitted. "I've assigned the case to the Main Crew, and am hoping they produce results soon."

Anger bubbled up inside me at that, and I had to force myself to let it go. I wanted to demand that Iannis let *me* handle the investigation, but I couldn't have that conversation with everybody else in the room, and besides, my plate was a little full with Sillara's case right now.

"Well in the meantime, don't you think we should do something to discourage shifters from buying the drugs?" I asked. "If we can't stop them from being sold, maybe we can stop them from being bought."

"What exactly do you have in mind?" Iannis asked, turning toward me, the interest clear in his voice.

"I'm not sure Miss Baine's suggestion would be effective, at least not in the long run." Director Chen commented. "Many shifters tend to be too impulsive to be easily deterred from the instant gratification narcotics provide." I bristled at the condescending undertone to her voice.

"Director Chen," Iannis warned, but before he could say any more, Lakin spoke up.

"What if we started an urban legend that these drugs cause impotence?"

"Huh." Elnos tapped his chin, sounding mildly impressed. "That would only work against the male population, but still, it would be a start."

"We could also spread a similar rumor about female infertility," I said. "Who's to say it's not true, anyway? Silver will kill us in large enough doses; exposure to small quantities over a large period of time could produce all kinds of harmful side-effects."

"That's very plausible," Elnos agreed, nodding. "It might even be true."

"Excellent," Iannis said. "Miss Baine and Inspector Lakin can spread the rumors, the sooner the better. In the meantime," he turned to Director Chen, "I expect you to check in regularly with the Main Crew on their progress."

"Yes sir." Director Chen bowed.

"Good. You are dismissed."

I turned to leave along with everyone else, but Iannis reached out and placed a hand on my bare shoulder. A tingle ran through my body at the skin on skin contact. "Wait."

"What is it?" I turned toward him, hoping that he wouldn't notice the blush stinging my cheeks. Iannis's violet gaze swept me from head to toe, briefly lingering on the hint of cleavage peeking out from beneath my tank top's neckline, and suddenly I wished I'd traded it in for something a little more loose-fitting.

"I wanted to ask about your progress regarding the banking scheme. Did your investigation turn up anything?"

"No." Annoyance flickered in my chest. "I've been a little pre-occupied." Truthfully I had completely forgotten about the bank – the shifter disappearances were more important, especially now that my cousin's daughter was one of the victims.

"Well get it done today," Iannis ordered. "You are running out of time."

"Fine." I wasn't really sure why the Chief Mage was being so insistent about this when we had bigger things to worry about, but I wasn't about to push my luck – he'd given me his trust when he allowed me to have the last few mornings off, and I needed to produce results or he wouldn't do it again. "I'll have a report to you by tomorrow morning."

"Excellent. You are dismissed."

I turned on my heel and left, hurrying to catch up with Lakin, who was already halfway down the hall.

"Hey," he said as I fell into step with him. "What was that all about?"

I sighed. "The Chief Mage asked me to look into the interest-free loans Sandin Federal Bank has been offering shifters," I told him. "He was just reminding me of my obligation, is all."

"Sandin Federal Bank?" Lakin frowned. "You don't say."

I arched my brows at the tone of his voice. "What aren't you telling me?"

"It could be nothing." But Lakin didn't sound so sure. "I went back to Nevin's house yesterday afternoon to search it a bit more thoroughly, and I found loan documents from Sandin Federal Bank in his files. Looks like he'd taken advantage of one of the interest-free loans."

"How long ago?"

"Last January, I think."

"Hmm." I pursed my lips. "So have lots of others. I'm not sure that's enough to make a connection."

"Still, it's worth checking out, especially if the Chief Mage holds them in suspicion." Lakin bumped my shoulder as we trotted down the front steps. "May as well kill two birds with one stone, right?"

"Good point."

Before making our way to Shiftertown we stopped by Sandin Federal Bank, which, as a human-owned facility, was located in the heart of Maintown. It was a large limestone building with a green tiled roof, the name of the company displayed proudly across the front in gold block lettering. Large windows set into the outer walls allowed in plenty of light, and through them I could see that it was just as big on the inside as it was on the outside, with five teller windows and a number of desks and offices where bankers and clerks could help customers apply for loans.

Soft music playing from a set of speakers greeted us as we walked in, along with the strong scent of rich coffee coming from a station set up near the doorway. The station boasted a coffee pot, a tray of mugs and a platter of cookies, an enticing incentive for prospective customers to hang out in the visitors' chairs and wait for one of the busy employees. And there were a lot of visitors, I noticed, glancing at the row of low red scoop chairs lining the wall to my left. Nearly all of them were occupied by shifters, and there were more people standing on the cream-colored tile of the lobby, also waiting for their shot at a loan.

"Good morning." A curvy brunette human in a dark red skirt suit approached us, her shoes clicking on the polished tile. Her hair was pulled back from her heart-shaped face in a sleek chignon, her make-up expertly done. "Welcome to Sandin

Federal Bank. My name is Aryn. Are you here to apply for one of our interest-free loans?"

"No," I said, holding up my Enforcer's bracelet before Lakin could speak. "We're actually here to talk to your manager. Is he available?"

Annoyance flashed in the woman's dark eyes, but she quickly covered it up with a warm smile. "I'm afraid Mr. Danrian is with a customer just now, but if you'd like to make an appointment –"

"Do you see this?" I demanded, shaking my wrist so that the bronze shield charm dangled in front of the woman's pert nose. "This means I don't need an appointment, and I don't need to wait. Tell Mr. Danrian that Enforcer Sunaya Baine and Shifter-town Inspector Boon Lakin are here to see him, *now*."

Aryn snapped her mouth shut. "Very well," she said curtly. "Please wait here a moment." She turned on her heel and walked briskly across the room, her hips swaying in time to the motion.

"Nice," Lakin murmured as he turned away to help himself to a cup of coffee. "You don't seem to have any problem being intimidating."

"It's a job requirement." Giving in to temptation, I snagged a chocolate-covered cookie from the platter, then popped the entire thing in my mouth so I wouldn't risk getting crumbs on my shirt. I wasn't going to walk into an interview with pieces of cookie on me – that was just unprofessional, especially when the cookies belonged to your suspect.

I turned around just as Aryn returned. "Mr. Danrian will see you now."

"Excellent," I quipped, mimicking the Chief Mage's tone. Lakin choked on his coffee next to me, and I bit back a grin as we followed Aryn to a corner office in the rear of the building. The walls were made entirely of glass, the privacy shades raised so that anyone passing by had a perfect view of the interior – and it was a nice interior, with gold-framed photographs hanging from the cream walls, and honey-wood furniture that glowed beneath the light streaming in through the bay window.

"Good morning," the manager said coolly, standing up from behind his acre-wide desk. He was wearing a tan-colored suit with a green linen shirt that was a few shades darker than his tie. "I'm Warin Danrian, the regional manager."

"I'm Shiftertown Inspector Lakin, and this is Enforcer Baine," Lakin said before I had a chance to respond – guess he was getting tired of me making the introductions. "We're investigating a crime, and we need to ask you a couple of questions."

"I see," Danrian said calmly, but he couldn't quite wipe the irritation from his expression. "Are they the kind of questions that couldn't have waited a few more minutes? I was in the middle of helping a client with an important business deal."

"One of those interest-free loans?" I asked lightly, plucking one of the packets of paperwork from a basket hanging from the wall to my left. "The ones that are so popular in Shiftertown these days?"

Danrian's eyes narrowed as a crafty gleam entered them. "If you two are interested, we can fill out preliminary paperwork today." He gestured to the packet in my hands.

"We are interested, but not for ourselves." Lakin took a seat in one of the visitor's chairs without invitation, and I followed suit. "Why don't you sit down, Mr. Danrian, so we can go over it?"

"Alright." The manager seated himself in the buttery leather chair behind his desk. "Well get on with it, then. What is this all about?"

Lakin pulled a photo from one of the many pockets of his coat. "Do you recognize this man?"

Something flashed in Danrian's eyes as he glanced down at

the photo, a dark skinned, dark haired man with Sandian features. "What about him?"

"His name is Nevin Rindar," Lakin said. "He's a reporter for the Shifter Courier. And he came to you for a loan back in January."

The manager scoffed. "January? Do you have any idea how many shifters we've helped with loans over the past six months? You can't expect me to remember all of them."

"But you do remember him, don't you?" I leaned forward to pin the manager with my gaze. "I saw your eyes when you looked at the photo – you recognized the face."

"It's vaguely familiar," the manager said stiffly. "It's possible that I helped him with a loan, or that any of my staff did so. As I said, we've helped out many shifters."

I scowled – he wasn't lying, my nose and my hearing told me that much, but I could tell he was dancing around something.

"I'm not sure how much your loan 'helped' Nevin Rindar," Lakin said pointedly. "He's gone missing in the last two months, vanished without a trace, possibly even dead."

"And that's my fault how?" Danrian demanded.

"I haven't said it is," Lakin said patiently. "But nevertheless, I would like to know more about these loans you're offering."

"And not just what you tell the public either," I snapped.

"I don't know what there is to tell," Danrian said, but sweat had broken out across his upper lip, and I could smell the lie.

"Listen, asshole." I slapped my hand on the polished wood of his desk to draw his attention. "I don't know if anyone's ever told you this, but it's not a good idea to lie to shifters. Especially ones who have the ability to throw you in jail for a night or two."

"Alright, alright!" Danrian cried. He swiped a hand across his square face. "What do you want to know?"

"Why are you offering such favorable terms to shifters specifically?" I demanded. "As far as I can tell you're not offering interest-free loans to humans or mages, which doesn't make sense because they have more money. What do you get out of signing shifters up?"

"We get bonuses for every shifter that signs up!" Danrian exclaimed. "Especially if they have houses or property to pledge as security. It's been a win-win situation on both ends ever since Sandin Federal Bank has started up the program. Hundreds of shifters have been signing up every day across the country!"

"Clearly," Lakin snapped, impatience burning in his reddish-yellow eyes, "but why? Why are you being offered incentives?"

"You'll have to ask the home office about that," the manager said stiffly. "They're the ones who've been sending out the orders."

"Oh, so it's some big mysterious hand pulling strings behind the curtain again?" I wrinkled my nose. This entire thing stank of the Benefactor's involvement – as with the silver murders, Yantz had been the instrument, but he'd been following someone else's orders.

Danrian's eyes flashed again. "I would suggest you watch your tone, Enforcer Baine. Sandin Federal Bank has some very powerful investors. It would be unwise to upset any of them with baseless accusations."

"Oh really?" I stood up, then flattened my palms on the desk as I leaned across it, shoving my nose into Danrian's face. The man's eyes widened, and he leaned back in his chair to put some distance between us. "Well you might have some bigwigs behind you, but I've got the Chief Mage behind me, and he's *very* inter-ested in your bank's activities, Mr. Danrian." I bared my teeth into a vicious grin. "If I were you, I'd be careful that you haven't 'accidentally' gotten yourself into anything illegal."

Danrian's cheeks mottled. "How dare you throw around accusations like that in my office!' He leapt to his feet. "Unless either of you plan on arresting me, I demand that you leave. Now."

"No worries," Lakin said, curling a hand into the fabric of my shirt and gently pulling me backward. "We've got another interview coming up, so we'll be on our way." He stood up, releasing my shirt as he did so. "We'll be back if we have more questions."

"Naturally," Danrian's voice was like ice. "I do wish you the best of luck in your investigation."

"Of course you do," I said as I followed Lakin out the door. I turned back for just a moment to wink at Danrian, who was watching us with a stony expression. "Have a nice day." *While it lasts,* I added to myself silently. I didn't know what Danrian was hiding from us yet, but I was going to find out, and once I did I was going to ruin his week.

12

After we left the bank, I asked Lakin to go off to Shiftertown without me to spread the impotence rumors, then turned my wheels in the direction of the Palace. This whole business with the bank was nagging at me, and while the Chief Mage would probably be too busy to go over it with me until tomorrow, there was someone else I could ask in the meantime.

I found Fenris in the Palace Library – a huge room that could have easily fit the entire Shifter Courier building inside the bookshelves that stood in rows in the middle of the room and lined the walls, so tall they nearly touched the soaring ceiling. He was sitting toward the front, buried in a dusty leather tome written entirely in Loranian, and I arched a brow. Not for the first time, I wondered how it was that Fenris was fluent in the magical language, when most shifters weren't. Yes, he spent a lot of time around Iannis, but I wasn't sure that explained it... not to mention that their friendship itself was highly unusual. Nobody seemed to question it, but it was unheard of for a mage of Iannis's rank to be such close friends with any shifter, especially a clanless one.

"Whatcha reading there?" I asked casually, wandering up beside him.

"Sunaya!" Fenris's head shot up, surprise flickering in his yellow eyes. Several of the mages sitting at the other tables shot us dirty looks for disturbing the silence of the library, and Fenris winced.

"Sorry," I muttered, lowering my voice as I sat down in the chair across from him. "Didn't mean to startle you. You must've really been into that book." That was the only explanation I could come up with – Fenris was a wolf shifter, and like me he had a heightened sense of smell and hearing. In his place I would have already known I was here before I'd spoken.

"Yes, well, it's fascinating stuff." Fenris closed the book gently, then pushed it to the side, spine facing away so that I couldn't read the title. I wondered if he'd done that on purpose, but now was not the time to ask – I'd just draw myself off-track, and it wasn't really my business anyway. "What are you doing back at the Palace? It's not even eleven o'clock, and it's not like you to be early."

"Gee thanks." I stuck my tongue out at Fenris, and he grinned a little. "Actually, I'm here because I was hoping you might be able to help me with the investigation the Chief Mage put me on earlier this week."

"You mean about the bank loans being given out to shifters?" Interest lit Fenris's dark eyes. "What can I do to help?"

"Well," I said, propping my elbows on the table and folding my hands beneath my chin, "Inspector Lakin and I went to Sandin Federal today to question the bank manager about the loans, and he said that hundreds of shifters have been signing up every day. But when I thought about it, I realized that's got to be a ridiculous amount of gold they're giving out. From what Lakin's heard around town the average loan amount is something like three hundred pieces of gold."

"That would be astronomical." Fenris's thick, black brows shot up. "And at zero percent interest? That certainly doesn't make any sense at all."

"No, it doesn't." I sighed, relieved that Fenris agreed with me. Finances weren't really my strong suit, and I'd been afraid I was just missing something. "So, where do you think they're getting that gold from?" As far as I knew, the money in circulation was produced by the Mages Guilds of each individual Federation state. "Is someone siphoning money from the Guilds?"

"I don't know how that would be possible." Fenris drummed his fingers on the table in thought, earning more dirty looks from the mages. But this time he ignored them. "The Mages Guilds in each state are only allowed to transmute a certain amount of coin every year. The quantity varies from state to state depending upon the local economy as well as Federation regulations, but that doesn't change the fact that there is a strict limit. If such large amounts of money were to go missing it would not go unnoticed."

"But don't you think it's possible one or more of the mages in charge of transmuting the coin could be making extra and setting it aside?"

"That would be high treason indeed." Fenris scowled. "The mage families have all pledged not to transmute gold, which is one of the laws laid down in the Great Accord, and in exchange they receive a handsome share of the year's allotment."

"Ugh. That is *so* unfair." I rolled my eyes, disgusted at the amount of privilege mages got simply for being born. "So in exchange for not producing anything, mages get handouts?"

"Yes, but they are required to spend it, and are not allowed to hoard more than ten percent of their yearly allotment."

"Oh, that makes me feel so much better."

"Sunaya, I'm not here to have a political debate. I'm just stating the facts."

"Right." I sucked in a breath through my nostrils, and then let it go. There was no point in arguing about this – Fenris hadn't made the law, after all, but I was surprised that he wasn't as incensed about it as I was, being a shifter himself.

Maybe he's just come to terms with it.

Huh. Well if that ever happened to me, I hoped someone did me a favor and put me out of my misery. I would *never* be okay with the current status quo.

"Fine," I finally said. "I get it. The mages don't want to risk losing their yearly allowance. But if they're not doing this, then who is?"

"I might have an idea about that." Fenris stood up, grabbing the book he'd been reading. "Here, let's go somewhere more private."

I followed him to a small table in the back, where no one else seemed to be sitting. Fenris settled into the chair across from me, then pulled a large money pouch from his belt. He emptied the pouch, sending gold, pandanum and bronze coins spilling across the table. I snagged one of them, envy twinging in my gut – clearly Fenris got way more of an allowance than I did. I guess it paid to be the Chief Mage's right-hand shifter, instead of just a lowly apprentice.

"What are we looking for, exactly?"

"Traces of magical residue," Fenris answered, picking up one of the coins and sniffing it. "These coins are all supposed to be transmuted by the Guild, and if that's the case then they should all smell like any object that's been changed by spellcraft."

Nodding, I held the coin to my nose. Sure enough, I detected a faint whiff of magic. Fenris and I went through the others, and it wasn't until I hit my tenth one that I noticed anything different.

"Huh," I muttered, sniffing the gold coin in my hand just to be sure. "This one doesn't smell like magic."

"Let me see." Eyes narrowed, Fenris held out a hand for the coin, and I pressed it into his palm. He sniffed it as well, and his lips thinned. "This coin wasn't produced by the Mages Guild."

"Then where was it produced?'

Fenris shrugged. "I can't say what foundry was used, but the metal was mined naturally, not transmuted, which is illegal under Federation law. It is also not easy, as most of the known mines are located on inaccessible tribal lands."

"Oh." My eyebrows arched at the implication. There were a number of indigenous tribes scattered across the Northia Federation, remnants of the civilization that used to exist here before people from across the Eastern Ocean had migrated over here, and taken over large parts of their lands. Mining was shunned by these tribes as they saw little to no use for precious stones and metals, and most of them guarded their territory fiercely. This benefitted the Federation, since they wanted to keep the mines off limits, and their citizens well away from temptation.

"Let's keep looking, and place any other such coins in a pile over there." Fenris placed the coin in his hand on the far end of the table, signifying where the pile should start.

By the time we finished going through all of Fenris's coins, we had small stack of illegal gold coins – five in total, out of eighteen. The number was alarming, and I wondered just how long this would have had to be going on for this many of the coins to get into circulation.

"Well, at least we know why the bank doesn't seem to have a problem giving away all this money," Fenris said, his lips thinning. "It's counterfeit."

"Is it?" I asked dubiously, holding up a gold coin. "I mean, it's made out of the same stuff, isn't it? Technically it should be even more valuable since it's the real thing and not mage-made. Not to mention it would still cost a pretty penny to produce, from the mining costs to the actual minting. I still don't see how banks could just afford to give this stuff away."

Fenris scowled. "Maybe so, but production of money like this is prohibited by law, and therefore the term 'counterfeit' still applies." He shook his head, chagrined. "The Mages Guild should be checking on this sort of thing, and regularly."

"I guess that's just one more thing to add to the list," I said dryly. It would be a lot easier if they hired a shifter to weed out counterfeits, but I doubted they would listen to me if I suggested it. Knowing my luck the stingy bastards might dump the job on me instead.

"Indeed." Fenris jumped to his feet, eyes sparking with ire, and I blinked. I'd never seen him this incensed before. "I will speak to Iannis about this at once. These pesky humans are getting out of hand, and this abuse needs to be stopped immediately. Good morning, Sunaya."

And with that, he strode out of the room, leaving me staring after him.

13

I spent the rest of the afternoon at the Mages Guild slogging through paperwork, so by the time I walked out the front doors of the Palace I was almost looking forward to the Shifter Royale. Maybe if I was going to watch mages instead of shifters I would have been more enthusiastic. It would probably be educational to watch a couple of mage duels, actually. But even if I wasn't thrilled about attending the Royale itself, I was looking forward to the opportunity of finding out whether or not the missing shifters were ending up in these illegal fights.

I parked my bike near my apartment, then changed into a tight black halter dress and a pair of ankle boots – the less I had to change myself for the illusion, the less magic I would have to expend. I then hoofed it over to the Enforcer's Guild, which was less than twelve blocks from where I lived. By the time I got there, Lakin and Annia were already standing by the front doors, chatting amicably enough. I arched my brows at the sight of the huge purple and white steamcar parked in the middle of the lot, ten feet from where they were standing.

"Well look at you," Lakin murmured as he caught sight of me, his reddish-yellow eyes looking me up and down. They lingered on the ample amount of cleavage I was showing, and I felt a blush sting my cheeks. "You clean up well."

"Thanks." I turned toward Annia, hoping to change the subject – encouraging Lakin's flattery really wasn't a good idea. "You borrowed your mom's car?"

Annia shrugged. "I figured it was easier than having all three of us show up on steambikes." She looped an arm around my waist, grinning a little as she tugged me close. "Besides, I don't want your hair getting messed up for our second date."

Lakin's brows shot up as I rolled my eyes. "Is there something I'm missing?" he asked.

"I had the bright idea that we should pretend to be a lesbian couple when we went to buy the tickets, so that it wouldn't be so weird that two girls were walking into a gambling club by ourselves." I swatted Annia's hand away. "Since so many people saw us, we have to keep up the ruse."

"Well that explains the dress," Lakin commented, and Annia raised her brows at the hint of jealousy in his voice. She gave me a questioning look, but dropped it when I jerked my head to the side emphatically. This was work, not a date, and we would play our roles accordingly. Annia had certainly done her part – she was wearing a biker's jacket, jeans and kick-ass boots, and her long hair was slicked back from her forehead, revealing a pair of small steel hoops that winked at the top of her left ear. No one was going to mistake her for a girly-girl.

We hopped into the steamcar, Annia and I taking the front seats and Lakin in the back. I waited until we were across the bridge before I put on my illusion, turning myself into the petite blonde again.

"Whoa," Lakin said when I turned around in my seat to look at him. "That's really, really weird."

"Yeah, well now it's your turn." I reached for him. "Give me your hand."

Lakin recoiled. "What?"

I huffed impatiently. "You can't go into an illegal shifter fighting ring as a shifter. I have to put a spell on you to make you look and smell human."

Lakin glared at my outstretched hand. "I'm not comfortable with having spells cast on me."

"Fine." I turned to Annia. "Stop the car."

"What?" Lakin demanded.

I twisted around in my seat to pin him with a glare. "If you're not going to do this, then I can't take you with us. This may be your investigation, Lakin, but if you walk in there as you are now you're going to fuck the whole thing up and then we'll never find those missing shifters."

Lakin glared at me for a long moment, but I didn't back down. I understood his fear of magic, but I couldn't allow that to jeopardize our recon mission. If he wasn't going to play by the rules, then he was going to have to go. Even if that meant I had to toss him into the bay.

Just when I thought that maybe Annia really *was* going to have to stop the car, Lakin finally lowered his gaze. "Alright," he said, holding out his hand. "I trust you."

"Thank you." A heavy weight settled onto my shoulders with those words – trust was a heavy burden to bear. Clasping my hand in his, I closed my eyes briefly, envisioning the illusion I wanted Lakin to wear. It wasn't strictly necessary to hold his hand, of course – magic could be done from a distance, without direct contact – but it was a little easier. A flow of warmth traveled from his hand to mine, but I ignored it, focusing on the spell as I murmured the words.

When I opened my eyes, the Lakin I knew was gone.

"Okay. What do I look like?" Lakin patted his hands over his face, and his eyes widened as he felt the softer cheekbones and the triangular jaw. "By Magorah, Sunaya. What did you do to me?"

Annia laughed as she eyed him from the rearview mirror. "Don't worry," she called, her eyes twinkling as I dug a compact mirror out of my purse and handed it to Lakin. "You're fine."

Lakin pursed his lips – which were fuller than his own – and narrowed his new cornflower-blue eyes as he studied his reflection. "You've made my face rounder, and my hair is black," he muttered.

"I changed your clothes too," I commented, and he jumped.

"What!" He looked down, noticing that he no longer sported his long leather coat. Instead he wore a green corduroy jacket, and loafers instead of boots. I'd left his shirt and jeans the same – they'd been pretty generic.

"Come on," I said, rolling my eyes at his outrage. "That coat you wear is really distinctive. I don't want to leave any chance that someone will put two and two together. Your coat is still on your body, and when I lift the spell you'll see it again."

Lakin just shook his head at me. "I can't get over this," he said. "I smell the magic around me, so I know you've done something, but the fact that I'm looking down at myself and I don't *see* myself –" he broke off. "If I think about this too much, it's going to drive me crazy."

"Well don't," I suggested, turning around so I could settle back into my seat. "Think happy thoughts, and enjoy the sunset while it's still here."

I let out a little sigh as I looked out the window, my mood sinking – but this time it had nothing to do with the Shifter Royale, and everything to do with the way Lakin had reacted to my magic. Over the last few months, I'd come to realize that magic was just as much a part of me as my beast, and that in order to have control of myself I had to accept both sides. Which meant that whoever I chose to let into my life had to be okay with both sides too.

Lakin had been nothing but kind and helpful to me – a refreshing change from the way the rest of the Jaguar Clan treated me. But I couldn't ignore how he instinctively recoiled from magic, just like almost every other full-blooded shifter. There was no way that I could be with Lakin, not beyond a one-night stand, and I didn't do one-night stands with people I worked with. Not unless he outgrew his fear of magic, and at his age that was highly unlikely.

So I couldn't have Lakin, and I couldn't have Iannis. Who did that leave me with? I'd yet to come across any other mage I could tolerate, and Lakin's fear of magic was the same reason I'd never gotten seriously involved with other shifters – there was no way to have a long-term relationship with a shifter and keep my magic a secret. Probably my best chance at finding a mate would be if I ran into another shifter-mage hybrid like myself... and seeing how rare we were, I doubted that was ever going to happen.

Yup. I definitely didn't have to worry about Melantha cursing my progeny, because I was never going to have any.

"So," Annia said as she turned onto the main road leading to Turain. "When were you going to tell us that you spent part of the other day hanging on the underside of Firegate Bridge and defusing a bomb?"

"Huh?" I jerked myself out of my melancholy thoughts to stare at Annia.

She regarded me with a dry look. "A couple of enforcers saw a black panther clinging to one of the beams beneath the bridge. We all heard about the attack on the Bridge and how the Chief Mage stopped it, but nobody in the news mentioned that you were involved. And neither did you."

"You helped the Chief Mage defuse the bomb beneath the

Bridge?" Lakin's voice was incredulous. "How did you manage that in beast form?"

"Teamwork." I kept it at that, remembering my promise to Iannis that I wouldn't talk about the strange magic he'd used to temporarily merge our souls together. "I didn't think to mention it because I was distracted by the case."

"But Naya, you're a hero," Lakin protested. "Don't you think you deserve some recognition for stopping a Resistance attack?"

"Honestly Lakin, that's the last thing I need. The Resistance, according to my cousin Rylan, is already unhappy that I got involved in the first place. If the papers make a thing about it, I'm sure they would feel obligated to retaliate against me publicly somehow."

"Hmph." Annia scowled at that. "I never liked the Resistance's methods. The more I hear about them, the more they sound like power-hungry terrorists. I'm not convinced we'd be better off with them at the helm than the mages."

My eyebrows flew up at the vehemence in Annia's voice. "I didn't realize you'd taken such a hard stance against the Resistance." Most humans were fans of the movement – they were better off than shifters, but they still didn't like the fact that mages held most of the power.

"Yeah, well I started looking into them a bit more ever since Noria declared that she wants to run off and join up with the local Resistance army." Annia tightened her grip on the steering wheel. "I've tried talking to her about it, but she doesn't listen. I may have to have Mom chain her up at night to keep her from leaving."

"I'm honestly not sure even that would work." Shaking my head, I glanced out the window at the mountains flanking the road on either side of us, which looked like they'd caught fire in the light of the dying sun. Guilt squirmed in my chest – Noria had initially wanted to be an enforcer, and Annia and I had both tried to dissuade her from that path because it was a dangerous line of work, and also because as a talented techno-geek we knew Noria was capable of so much more. But when I'd been arrested and nearly executed for possessing illegal magic, Noria had been exposed to the corruption in the Enforcer's Guild, and decided the Resistance was the only group that had the power to right the scales. I couldn't help but feel that it was my fault Noria wanted to join the Resistance – if I hadn't fucked up and exposed my magic to everyone, she might still want to be an Enforcer. As much as the job sucked sometimes, it was better than joining a terrorist rebel army. At least being an enforcer didn't make you an enemy of the state, and though the system was flawed you still had the potential to do a lot of good.

"Yeah, well I'm planning on talking to her about the attack on the bridge the next time I see her," Annia declared. "Maybe that will knock some sense into her."

I sure hoped so. Because Noria was going to be finishing college soon, and if we didn't find something else to divert her attention to she might be gone by the time next semester came around.

We arrived in Turain just as night began to fully settle over the sky, and it took us a few minutes to find the address that Silon had given to Annia when she'd bought the tickets. Eventually, we rolled into a lot on which a large grey warehouse sat, the windows blacked out or boarded up. There were already a number of steambikes and steamcars parked in the lot, and I could make out a bouncer near the door, checking tickets and ushering prospective spectators inside.

"If I was going to be setting up an illegal fighting ring, I'd definitely pick a place like this," Lakin murmured.

"No kidding," Annia said, and I privately agreed. This building was located in Turain's industrial district, and there would be very little foot traffic here even during the day.

"Well, I guess we'd better get in there." I sucked in a long breath through my nostrils to steady myself, then squared my shoulders and climbed out of the vehicle. Lakin automatically stepped forward to help me down, but Annia beat him to it, taking my hand and then sliding her arm possessively around my waist.

"Lesbian couple, remember?" I whispered.

"Right," Lakin muttered as he followed us from behind. I could feel his eyes on my ass the entire time, and tried to ignore the sensation. When we were through with this I was going to have to give Lakin a stern talking-to – he was starting to show signs of possessiveness, and if I didn't nip it in the bud his shifter instincts were going to take over. I needed to remind his beast that he did *not* own me, and soon.

But right now we had bigger things to worry about.

"Tickets?" the bouncer growled, staring down at us through narrowed eyes. He was built like a bull, thickset but sturdy, and he wore his long brown hair in a tail that hung down to a waist easily three times the width of mine. Tattoos covered his forearms, and I resisted the urge to arch a brow. They were a bit of a rarity – mages shunned them, shifters couldn't have them, and the humans didn't consider them to be a respectable form of adornment.

"Coming right up." Annia dug into the pocket of her jeans and handed them to the bouncer. "Three tickets, three people."

The bouncer studied the tickets for a moment, then ripped off the stubs and handed them to us. "Head across the first floor to the far left corner and down the stairs. There'll be someone there to guide you."

We did as the bouncer said, our boots scuffing against the dusty concrete floor as we crossed the room. The space was largely empty except for a few rusted-out typesetting machines that stood like solitary islands in a sea of concrete, and I figured this warehouse had probably been owned by a major newspaper at some point. It reminded me of the Shifter Courier's dilapidated building, and I bit my lip. Maybe sometime tomorrow I would give the Chief Editor a call and tell him about the Shifter Royale.

Another human waited at the doorway on the other side of the room, this one smaller and leaner than the bouncer, but similarly muscular and no less intimidating. I could already hear the buzz of excited conversation even before he led us down the set of stairs, and an amalgam of scents wafted up to me – humans and shifters, reeking of a combination of excitement, fear and anger.

"I don't like this," Lakin growled in my head.

"You and me both."

We reached the basement, and I squinted against the harsh lights set into the ceiling; a bold contrast to the dusky sky outside. Annia took my hand, and I followed her blindly, waiting for my eyes to adjust to the light as the human led us down the stairs.

When my vision finally cleared, I had to bite back a gasp of shock.

Down here, beneath the abandoned warehouse, a huge fighting cage had been set up – a boxing ring that was surrounded by a silver-coated bamboo cage. There were bars set far enough apart to allow spectators to see inside, but close enough that they would impede anyone who tried escaping the ring. Rows of bleachers had been set up along three of the walls, and were already packed with excited humans, talking and laughing amongst each other as they waited for the fights to start. A couple of humans wearing bright red and white striped aprons wandered between the bleachers, offering popcorn and candy to the spectators in exchange for coin. Across the room, I could see a stocky man with long blonde hair dressed in a dark brown coat and hat talking to a human couple. He scribbled something in the beat-up leather book in his hands, and the couple handed him a coin. That must be one of the bookies.

But none of this was the shocking part.

On the far right, away from the bright lights and the bleachers, about ten different shifters crouched in cages, all in human form. Their colorful shifter eyes were tinged with red, and ropes of drool hung from their snarling mouths, making them look crazed. Anger sizzled in my gut at the sight of shackles gleaming at their wrists, and as I looked closer I could see glowing runes inscribed into the metal Those shackles must be keeping them from shifting – their beasts were all so close to the surface that I couldn't see any other reason why they wouldn't already be in animal form. The shackles looked similar to the ones that had been placed on me to prevent me from using my magic after I was arrested, and my stomach roiled in remembered anguish.

Annia squeezed my hand, hard, and it took me a second to realize that I'd been growling. Snapping my mouth shut, I turned my head away from the horrible sight and continued to follow our host. He led us to the bleachers on the far side of the room, closest to the shifter cages, and gestured for us to go sit on the second row.

"Those are your seats," he said. "Get settled in – we're about to start."

"Thank you," Annia said, and the human left us. We clambered up the bleachers, squeezing past the humans already seated and earning ourselves numerous glares as we bumped a few elbows. But I didn't care – these humans were complicit in helping some sick bastard profit off the misery of the shifters in those cages.

"Why do you think their eyes are red?" Annia murmured as she settled herself in between me and Lakin. Her dark eyes scanned the room casually, and I knew she was checking for threats and escape routes. There didn't really seem to be any way out of this place aside from the staircase we'd entered through, but I wondered if maybe there was a hidden door we were missing. It seemed like it would be too difficult for them to transport all the shifters down through that stairwell, and I doubted they kept the shifters here when the fights weren't taking place.

"They'll be drugged to the max," Lakin muttered tightly, keeping his eyes fixed on the stage. I had a feeling he was ignoring the shifters on purpose to try and keep his emotions in check. "All the addicts I've taken in recently had bloodshot eyes like that."

"Right." An image flashed in my mind of a crazed rhino shifter charging me, blood flowing from his flared nostrils, and I shuddered a little. That was the day my life had changed forever – the day I'd rushed into a rabbit shifter's house in Rowanville to try and save her babies from a rampaging rhino shifter who'd decided to attack her family for no good reason. I'd ended up incinerating him with a magical blast to stop him from killing me, but before that had happened I'd gotten a good look at his eyes, and they'd been bloodshot too. We couldn't be sure since I'd turned him into a pile of ash, but I was pretty certain he'd been on the shifter drugs too.

"Shit!" Annia cursed under her breath, nudging me. "We've got company. Brin and Nila are here."

I stiffened at the names of the two human enforcers who'd been assigned to Roanas's case, and who'd done absolutely nothing to solve it. Not only had those two assholes arrested me when they'd found out I had magic, they'd also stolen my crescent knives and chakrams and sold them off. If the Chief Mage hadn't tracked my weapons down, I would never have gotten them back.

Following Annia's gaze, I saw Brin, a tall, muscular man with bronze hair and good looks, and Nila, a petite blonde with huge boobs that probably netted her more bounties than her actual fighting skills. They were scanning the crowd with watchful eyes, and my heartbeat ratcheted up as I realized what would happen if they saw Annia.

"Do something!" she hissed in my ear. "Give me a disguise, like you did with Lakin."

"Okay." I scooted myself closer to Annia and snuggled in, nuzzling her neck with my nose. The smelled of patchouli and soap teased my nostrils as I reached for my magic and murmured the Words of the illusion spell. I couldn't change Annia's appearance completely, not in the middle of a crowd like this, so I focused on the little things, making her a little shorter, a little thicker in the waist and thighs, and dulling her features so that they weren't so attractive. For good measure, I gave her a slightly bulbous nose and pudgy cheeks.

"What exactly did you do to me?"

"I just made you look like your older, unattractive sister. If you had one, that is."

"Great."

"Just pretend to be from out of town somewhere if you talk to them."

"They've got to be paid off somehow," Annia murmured as she turned her face to bury it in my hair. "I'm sure they're not just here for fun, judging by the way they're surveying the room. They're making sure no one's here who isn't supposed to be."

"Oi." A gruff voice caught our attention. "You taking bets?"

We glanced down to see the bookie standing just below us, his leather book clutched in his hand as he stared up at us expectantly. My jaw clenched at the idea of putting money down on the lives of any of those caged shifters, but I knew we had to or we would look suspicious, so I turned my attention back toward the cages, studying the "contestants". At this distance I couldn't tell what all of them were, but I knew they were all predators of some kind – I spotted a wolf, a tiger and a lion amongst the bunch.

"I don't think we got a line-up of the fights," Annia said coolly, holding out a hand.

The bookie's eyes narrowed, but he dug into his pocket and pulled out a list, then handed it to Annia. Lakin and I leaned in so we could scan the matches – five total. I let out a little sigh of relief – this wasn't an elimination contest. I wasn't sure if I could manage to sit through that many fights.

Annia put her bet on the gray wolf in "wolf vs. lion", and Lakin decided to back the wolverine going up against the grizzly bear.

"You gonna place a bet?" the bookie asked me.

"Oh I don't like betting." I giggled, leaning my shoulder against Annia's and batting my lashes at the man. "I've never really been good with odds. I leave that sort of thing to her." I squeezed Annia's arm.

"Suit yourself." The bookie shrugged, then closed his book and moved off.

I sighed in relief as I watched him walk away, partially because I didn't have to bet and also because I really didn't have any money to put down anyway.

"You seem to be getting pretty good at playing the bimbo card," Annia teased me under her breath.

My lips quirked up in a brief smile. "It's the only card I've got at my disposal right now, so I may as well take advantage of it."

The announcer, a skinny man in a flashy green suit with a shock of bright orange hair, got up onto his podium and picked up his microphone. "Ladies and gentlemen, welcome to the Shifter Royale!" he cried, and the crowd went wild. I forced myself to clap and cheer with all the others, and Annia and Lakin followed suit. "Thank you all for coming tonight! We've got a fantastic line-up for you this evening, so I hope you've all placed your bets. Are you ready to get started?"

"YEAHHHH!" The audience shouted, and I fought the urge to clap my hands over my ears at the deafening roar.

"Then let's begin! First up, a real classic here at the Shifter Royale – Grizzly Bear versus Polar Bear!"

I watched as two of the cages were opened, and the shifters were dragged out. They tried to bite and snap at their handlers, but the humans who pulled them from their cages were well trained – they used a strange clamping device to grab the shifters by their throats and drag them out, and then each shifter was grabbed by two humans, with four more standing by as backup, and hauled to doors on opposite sides of the ring. It wasn't until the shifters were inside that the humans unlocked their handcuffs, and then beat a hasty retreat as the shifters instantly started changing.

My heart pounded as I watched the white light engulfing the two males as their shapes stretched and reformed, until two hulking bears stood on opposite ends of the ring. They both let out eardrum-shattering roars, then charged each other, battle fever raging in their bloodshot eyes. Claws sank into fur as the bears grappled for the upper hand, their heads twisting as they tried to bite each other. The polar bear managed to get his maw around the grizzly's more accessible ear, and the tang of blood laced the air as he ripped at it with his fangs. The grizzly roared again, struggling, but the pain threw him off balance and he toppled to the ground, the polar bear on top of him. It wasn't long before the polar bear clamped his jaw around the grizzly's neck, teeth sinking into the thick fur as he tried to tear out his opponent's windpipe.

"And we have a winner!" the announcer cried. "Polar bear comes out on top!" The crowd went wild, a mixture of cheers and boos, and I clenched my fists – that polar bear was going to kill the grizzly if someone didn't do something!

Thankfully, someone did – the announcer made a gesture, and two humans came forward, both holding some kind of long, tubular device. They pointed them at the bears and shot them with some kind of dart. Instantly, both bears went limp, collapsing against the stained white surface of the ring, and to my shock, white light enveloped them as they shifted back to human form.

"What the fuck?" Annia muttered as we watched several humans rush into the ring so they could re-cuff the shifters and drag them back to their respective cages. "How the hell did they manage to force unconscious shifters to change?"

"It's got to be some kind of magic," I hissed, unable to hold back my glare as I stared at the now-empty ring. "There's no way some drug did that on its own. There's a mage involved somewhere."

Just like there'd been a mage involved in the Resistance's attack on the bridge. One strong enough to strip away the wards.

I froze as I considered that. The substance they'd used to attach the bomb to the underside of the bridge had been magical in nature, just like whatever the humans had just injected those shifters with. It was one thing for humans to use charms and potions, but the magic involved at the bridge and the injections given to those shifters were really powerful and sophisticated. What mage of that stature would be willing to work with humans like this? Was it possible the same mage that had been involved in the attack on the bridge was also involved with this? I couldn't see respectable mages working for the Resistance, but it was possible they might have roped in some renegade who was unhappy with the current regime. I supposed it could also be a witch, but if that were the case they would have to be an unusually powerful one.

"*This is disgusting,*" Lakin spat, disturbing my train of thought. "*I can't believe we're just sitting here and watching this happen!*" A muscle ticked in his jaw.

"*We could always try talking to them,*" I said dubiously as I glanced at the maddened shifters snarling in their cages. "*Maybe get some information that could help us stop this*".

"*Already tried that,*" Lakin growled. "*They're unresponsive, the lot of them. Full of blood lust.*"

For three more fights, we watched shifter after shifter get thrown into that horrible cage and forced to fight each other. The drugs pumping through their system made them ferocious – they didn't even think twice about attacking each other once they were free of their shackles and thrown into the ring. The humans ate it up of course – they shouted and cheered and threw popcorn and apple cores at the shifters, as if the beasts fighting in the cage weren't living, breathing beings that deserved respect and freedom. It made me sick to my stomach, both the inhumanity of the situation and the effort it took to hold back the emotion that kept trying to burst out of me.

"Alright, ladies and gentlemen!" the announcer cried after the last two shifters – a cougar and a wolf – were dragged off the stage and returned to their cages. "And now for our final match, I offer you a treat! Lion versus tiger, in a fight to the death!"

Horror rushed through me, propelling me to my feet, and I nearly jumped off the bleachers before I remembered myself. Luckily, the rest of the crowd surged to their feet with cheers and whoops, so my cover wasn't blown. Blood pounded hot and heavy in my ears as I stared at the ring, watching as the lion and tiger shifters were tossed inside. My heart twisted as I watched the tiger – a female – struggle to her feet, her long hair matted and the bags under her eyes so deep they looked like smudged charcoal. Whatever they'd been pumping these shifters up with was clearly hitting her harder than the male she was facing, who'd already started to change. I could tell the woman was struggling to reach for her beast, but it wasn't happening.

He's going to rip her to shreds.

A wave of helplessness washed over me as I watched the glow fade from around the lion shifter's form, and I clenched my trembling hands into fists. I felt so useless, so ashamed. Who was I to call myself an enforcer, if all I could do was stand by and watch as one of my own kind was murdered?

You are not just a shifter, Sunaya Baine, a voice murmured in my head. *You are also a mage, and it is your birthright to use your magic to protect the weak.*

I started, not just at the unfamiliar voice in my head, but at the way the air around me changed – it grew lighter somehow, reminding me of the air inside Resinah's temple. I didn't know if it was she who spoke to me but the words filled me with strength, and my doubts and fears fell away. I wasn't helpless – I had the power to help these victims, and damned if I wasn't going to use it.

Reaching for my magic, I focused all my attention into the center of the ring, willing the illusion in my mind to form. Two seconds later, a towering flame sprang to life right between the two combatants, licking the ceiling with its long, colorful tongue. The lion shifter, who was about to pounce, shrank back, and the crowd's cheers turned to terrified shrieks as the fire began to spread.

Of course the fire wouldn't actually burn them, but they'd feel the heat and smell the smoke as if it really were.

The humans in charge of the Royale rushed to contain the shifters, a few of them throwing sand on the flames to try and put them out. I allowed the illusion to die down before the humans realized the fire wasn't real, and leapt from the bleachers as everyone else stampeded for the exits. I tried to make a run for the cages, but Annia grabbed the back of my dress and yanked me back.

"Get ahold of yourself, Naya," she growled. "You'll blow our cover for sure!"

I snarled, spinning around to confront her, but the velocity of the stampeding crowd forced me to either follow her or get trampled. People pushed and elbowed each other as the crowd clogged outside the stairwell, and I glanced back once more at the shifters stuck in their cages. They were already being moved out of the room by the few staff members who weren't corralling the spectators into an orderly evacuation, through a panel that had been slid open at the corner of the far wall when we weren't looking.

Guess we weren't allowed to use it as an emergency exit.

I wanted to turn around and investigate the secret entrance so badly it was a physical ache in my chest, but I knew Annia was right. If I did anything more now it would only blow our cover and possibly get us, and the shifters, killed. No, it was better to get an actual team of enforcers, ones who weren't being bribed, to come in here and arrest everyone. Until then, we had to pretend we were normal humans just like everyone else.

Once we made it to the upper floor of the warehouse, things calmed down a bit. Members of the event staff worked to direct the flow of traffic to the various exits, and they managed to gather everyone into the lot outside of the front of the building.

"Ladies and gentlemen!" The announcer called, standing up on the hood of a steamcar to make himself visible. "We apologize profusely for that rude interruption of tonight's Royale. Our staff has managed to put the fire out, so there is no need to call the fire department. If anyone is injured, please head over to the front – we have professionals who will render you first aid. For the rest of you, we are giving out free tickets to our next Royale as compensation for the abrupt end to this evening's entertainment. For those of you who are interested, please go and see Solin Endeman over there." The announcer pointed to his right, where Solin, the man who'd sold us the tickets, stood waiting.

About half of the crowd surged toward Solin, eager to claim tickets, but quite a few of the humans shook their heads and turned to leave, muttering amongst themselves. From the snippets of conversation I overheard, it didn't sound like they were planning on coming back to the Royale, and weary satisfaction briefly swept through me. Maybe I hadn't been able to rescue those shifters tonight, but I'd put a dent in the Royale's operation, and that would have to be enough to tide me over until I could crush them completely.

A handful of the attendees had been injured in the evacuation, trampled or smashed into walls, and those were led over to where Brin and Nila stood with a few other humans, a table with medical supplies set up. Brin looked like he'd been hurt, maybe by one of the shifters – Nila was binding his right forearm up with a length of gauze. My hands clenched into fists again, and I took a step toward them.

"Wait." Annia placed a hand on my shoulder. "Let me go and talk to them. I can help out with the first aid and see if I can get anything from those two. You, on the other hand, don't look like you've changed a bandage in your life, so you should wait for me here with Lakin."

"Fine." I wrinkled my nose at the accusation – I'd changed plenty of bandages, thank you very much – but I was playing the part of wimpy female tonight, so I hung back and watched as Annia made her way toward Brin and Nila. She introduced herself as an enforcer from a neighboring town, and after answering a couple of pointed questions Brin and Nila seemed to accept her.

"That was incredible, what you did back there with the fire," Lakin murmured in my ear from behind me. I shivered a little at the sensation of his warm breath on my neck, and turned my body at a three quarter angle so that I could see both him and Annia and also put some distance between us. "It was an illusion, wasn't it?"

"Yes." I looked up into Lakin's eyes, and felt a pang in my chest at the admiration I saw there. I wanted to lean into that gaze, to soak up the affinity and the admiration my soul craved, but I knew I couldn't trust that look. "I wasn't going to start a real fire, especially not in such a small space."

"Well you saved that tigress's life." Lakin squeezed my shoulder as he smiled down at me. "We may not have been able to free those shifters tonight, but you made sure that none of them died."

"I was just doing my job."

"No. You were just being you."

Warmth flooded through me, and I turned away before Lakin could catch the blush on my cheeks. Annia was crouched down in front of a human, bandaging up his ankle as she talked to Nila, and I tuned in on their conversation, hoping they were talking about something useful.

"... amazing, the way you guys manage to keep the shifters under control like that," Annia was saying. "Haven't any of them lashed out and killed someone?"

"Oh, that happened once or twice in the early stages," Nila said casually, as if she were talking about training a puppy who still hadn't learned not to pee in the house. "But we've been doing this for a couple months now, and we've got those shifters under control."

"How do you manage to get them here in the first place?" Annia asked. I was impressed at the admiration in her voice – if I didn't know better I would have thought she was actually praising Nila. "I can't imagine they're happy to be here or that they came voluntarily."

"They're not happy to be here," Brin said with a smirk. "But they only have themselves to blame. They should have been more careful about who they decided to default on their obligations to."

"Indentured servitude?" Lakin hissed, drawing the same conclusion I did from Brin's insinuation. "That's not only barbaric, but illegal!"

I agreed, but something more important was rolling through my mind. "Lakin, Brin said that the shifters here all defaulted on obligations. Do you think those obligations could be financial?"

Lakin narrowed his eyes. "I suppose. What are you suggesting?"

"There's a certain bank that's been offering interest-free loans to shifters," I said dryly.

Lakin's eyes widened. "You mean Sandin Federal? Do you really think such a reputable bank would be involved in a dirty scheme like this?"

I shrugged. "Just because they're interest-free doesn't mean they're payment-free. It's possible that the shifters they took just couldn't keep up with the payments."

Except for Mika, a voice in my head reminded me. *She was taken because of you.*

"Alright," Annia called, and I turned my head to see her walking back toward us. "Let's head home."

We all climbed into the purple and white steamcar in silence, the tension thick in the air as I waited for someone to stop us. But no one even spared us a second glance. Still, I held my breath until we were out onto the road, and didn't relax until we were far from Turain's industrial district.

"So," Annia finally said. "You got everything Nila and Brin told me?"

"Yeah. Debt slavery." I pressed my lips together. "I'd be interested to know who the investor is behind this, if we're right about what Brin is saying."

"And also why they're giving out loans to these shifters," Lakin interjected. I could see him scowling through the rearview mirror. "I interviewed nearly every one of those families, and none of them looked like they were in the position to take on a loan. Why would an investor extend credit to someone who almost certainly can't pay it off?"

"It almost sounds as if the investor, whoever they are, is trying to get these shifters indebted to him on purpose."

"But why?" I demanded. "So that he can force them into an illegal fighting ring? I don't know about you, but that sounds like an expensive way to get labor. He'd probably save more money if he just kidnapped them straight off."

"I don't know if it's about saving money," Annia said slowly. "I think it's about control."

"What do you mean?"

"I read something in a history textbook, back during my brief stint as a college student, that sounds kind of similar to this." Annia drummed her fingers on the steering wheel. "Two centuries ago, Garai was giving out loans to some of its smaller neighboring countries in the East, countries that were struggling with their own economies already. They ate up the gold greedily, of course, but they didn't fix their broken economic system and ended up being unable to pay back the debt. Garai used that as leverage to extort supplies, mages, and various favors from these countries, and eventually they were assimilated into their own country."

"Well that explains why Garai is so huge," I muttered. It was the largest country on the Eastern continent.

"I wonder if all the shifters who owe this investor money are being forced to fight in the Royale like this, or if this mysterious investor is extorting them in other ways." Lakin's eyes sharpened. "I'm going to have to interview friends and families again first thing in the morning and find out if they borrowed any money from Sandin Federal, and if so, whether they've been harassed by their creditor recently. Out of those twenty names on the list something ought to pop eventually."

"You want some help dividing that list up?" Annia asked. "Would probably be faster if you split up the workload."

Lakin hesitated. "I can always divide it up amongst my deputies."

"Not this time." I twisted around in my seat to face Lakin. "We could have gone to the Royale without you, Lakin, but I brought you in. The least you could do is let us help with the interviews in return."

"Alright," Lakin agreed. "Meet me at my house at eight in the morning. We need to get an early start on this, before any more shifters are taken."

"Sounds like a plan." I turned in my seat, settling my eyes on the Firegate Bridge as we approached it from around Hawk Hill. We were going to get to the bottom of this tomorrow, even if that meant I had to play hooky and piss the Chief Mage off all over again.

14

*A*nnia and I showed up at Lakin's house at eight in the morning, and we split up, Annia taking half of the phone call list, Lakin and me taking the other. At first I'd protested not having my own list, but Lakin insisted and I relented. After all, this was his case, not mine.

"So," I said as I settled onto my steambike. "Where are we headed first?"

"We're going to visit Tyron and Myrna Laniren."

"Laniren?" I echoed, racking my brain for the familiar name. "Wait, aren't those Tylin's parents? The wolf shifter from the local pack?"

"That's right." Lakin started up his engine. "I thought it would be good for you to see them for yourself, since it was their son's disappearance that sparked Sillara's investigation."

"Well that's very thoughtful of you."

Lakin grinned before putting his helmet on. "I try."

The wolf clan was located on the west side of Shiftertown, closer to the heart of the city. Small, wood-framed houses lined the streets, some in better condition than others, and because it was summer there were many shifter children out on the sidewalks and the front yards, laughing and playing. Their mothers stared watchfully at us from their front porches, colorful shifter eyes narrowed on our bikes as we passed. Most shifters didn't own bikes or cars – for one, vehicles were expensive, and for shifters they weren't really necessary as many of them could travel just as fast in beast form. The children stared wide-eyed at our bikes as we zipped by, curiosity and excitement on their little faces, and it reminded me of how excited I'd been when I'd first laid eyes on a steambike myself. I'd been sixteen years old, tagging along on an errand with Roanas in Rowanville when a trio of enforcers had shot out of the Guild parking lot riding steambikes. I'd been transfixed by the vehicles, with their large wheels and shiny handlebars, and the way the riders moved so fast on them, leaving nothing but clouds of hot steam in their wake. It had taken me six years, from that very point on, to save up for my own bike, and I loved it to death.

The Laniren house was at the top of a hill – a small, two-bedroom dwelling with white siding and robin's egg blue shutters and roofing tile. I narrowed my eyes as we parked across the street from the house – the paint looked new, the tiles freshly laid, unlike many of the houses we'd passed.

"Looks like the Lanirens have spruced up their house a bit," I commented.

Lakin's eyes narrowed as he nodded. We crossed the street, and the woman playing in the front yard with her toddler froze at our approach, her pale-blue wolf shifter eyes narrowing on me.

"Good morning, Mrs. Laniren," Lakin greeted her as she stood, scooping her toddler up and propping the child on her hip. "This is my associate, Enforcer Baine. We'd like to speak with you and your husband, if that's possible."

"I know who you are," Myrna said, her eyes still focused on me. She was a pretty woman, with long, curly brown hair and a decent figure wrapped up in a simple green dress, but the look in her eyes as she stared at me was downright ugly. "You're the hybrid, the one in favor with the Chief Mage. What would you care about my son's disappearance?"

"The enforcer who was working on your case, Sillara Tarenan, was a friend of mine," I said coolly, ignoring the scorn in Myrna's eyes. "We believe she was killed for looking into your son's disappearance, and I have a vested interest in finding her killer, so I'm helping Inspector Lakin out today. I hope you don't mind."

"Well, I'm afraid my husband isn't home today." The toddler on her hip babbled, reaching a hand out toward me as she stared up at me, and Myrna shifted her stance, putting distance between me and the baby. The blatant show of distrust stung, and I forced my gaze away from the baby's wide blue eyes. "He's working, and will be until dinner."

"That's quite alright, Mrs. Laniren," Lakin said smoothly. "We can just talk to you in the meantime. Is there somewhere more private we can go?"

Tears suddenly filled Myrna's eyes. "You... you're not here to give me bad news, are you? My son isn't dead. He can't be dead!" Her already pale cheeks turned a dead white.

"No, no of course not." Lakin placed a soothing arm on Myrna's shoulder. "We're just trying to run down a lead that may help us with your son's whereabouts, and I need to ask you a few more questions."

"Very well." Myrna sniffed, then turned around. "Come this way."

She led us inside, and my eyes narrowed as I studied the interior. The granite countertop separating the kitchen to my left from the rest of the living room looked fairly new – it was blemish-free and sparkling, as were the refrigerator, stove and cabinets. Of course that could possibly be attributed to Myrna's cleaning skills; she could just be really good at maintaining her house.

But the living room beyond boasted fairly expensive looking furniture – stuffed couches, gleaming oak side tables, a thick Garaian rug... and the hardwood floor that creaked beneath my feet looked new.

"Can I get you anything?" Myrna asked Lakin with a tired sigh as she set her daughter down in a playpen set up alongside the wall. The little girl instantly plopped down onto her butt and reached for a stuffed wolf to play with.

"No, we're fine," Lakin assured her. He allowed his eyes to play across the furniture as we sat down on a dark green love seat, as if he hadn't already taken in the surroundings. "You have a very nice home, Mrs. Laniren."

"Thank you." A brief smile lightened Myrna's face, taking off a few years. Since shifters normally lived to around three hundred, we aged much more slowly than humans, but stress could still take a toll on our looks. "We had everything redone a few months ago and I've worked hard to maintain it. Which isn't as easy as it sounds when you have a toddler around." She glanced fondly at her child, and pity stirred in my chest. It was clear she loved her son as much as she did her daughter – it was probably killing her that he was gone.

"That must have been quite expensive."

Myrna sighed again. "It was." Lines tightened around her pale blue eyes as she, too, looked around the room. "We never really intended to fix up the entire house, but the pipes were rusting and the roof badly needed repair, and when rats started chewing through our electrical wiring... oh, it was just horrible." She dragged her hands through her curly hair. "If Tyron hadn't gotten us that loan, I don't know what we would have done with the house."

"Loan?" I asked, my heart leaping as Myrna confirmed my suspicions. "Where did you get the loan from?"

"Sandin Federal Bank." Myrna narrowed her eyes at me. "Why do you ask?"

"Have you been keeping up with your loan payments, Mrs. Laniren?" Lakin asked.

"Of course!' Myrna's face flushed. "We're responsible people. We wouldn't take on a debt that we couldn't pay." But Lakin and I could both smell the lie, and she knew it.

"Mrs. Laniren, nobody is trying to judge you," Lakin said soothingly. "We're just trying to get more information. Are you sure that you were keeping up with your payments? You never missed any, not even one?"

Myrna sighed. "Well, we did miss a *few* of them, but never two in a row, and we always tried to pay extra the following month to keep up. It happens to everyone, doesn't it?"

"Of course," Lakin said smoothly. "Did you ever receive any threatening communication from the bank when you missed the payments? Phone calls, letters?"

"I don't understand. Why are you asking all this?"

"Some information has recently come to light," I butted in, impatient to cut to the chase. "Information suggesting that all of the families of the recent kidnapping victims may have been struggling with debt payments. We're trying to see if there might be some connection, something that could lead us to the kidnapper, and aside from the fact that you're all shifters, the debt problems are the only common theme we're finding."

The blood drained from Myrna's face. "Are you saying that Tylin was taken from us because we weren't making our payments?"

"We can't be sure," Lakin said gently. "But we're not ruling it out, either."

The color abruptly rushed back into Myrna's face, turning

her skin bright red. "I *knew* we never should have taken on that loan!" she growled, jumping to her feet. She bared her fangs as she began pacing back and forth across the rug, her expression livid. "I'm going to kill Tyron when he gets home!"

The toddler let out a distressed wail at the sound of her mother's voice, and Myrna's expression softened as she dropped down to her knees in front of the playpen to scoop up her daughter.

"Don't worry, Liv," she cooed, rocking the small child. "Mommy's okay. You don't need to be upset." She dropped a kiss on the top of her daughter's curly head and I heard her whisper, "I'm just so glad I still have you here."

My heart ached at the pain in her voice, and for once I was glad to be unattached – I couldn't imagine what it would be like if I had a child and he was taken from me. I may not have been a mother, but the maternal instinct stirred inside me at the sight of this woman's pain, and for a moment I wanted to comfort her.

But I didn't, because I knew she wouldn't accept comfort, not from an outcast like me.

"So was it your husband's idea to seek out a loan in order to make the repairs on your house?" Lakin asked.

Myrna placed her toddler back in the playpen, then turned toward us, a simmering anger burning behind her eyes. "Yes, it was Tyron's idea to take advantage of the interest-free loans being advertised. He was initially only going to take out enough money to fix the bare necessities, but Sandin Federal offered him five times the amount, and it was more money than Tyron and I had ever seen in our lives. I couldn't find it in me to be angry when he came skipping home with that pouch of gold in his hand. But I'm angry now." Her lower lip trembled as she clenched her fists. "If I'd known that money was going to bring tragedy down on my family, I would have made him return it right away."

"So did you receive any threats from Sandin Federal?" I asked. "Anything beyond the usual late payment notices?"

Myrna hesitated. "Not at first, no, and never directly. But there were a few times I heard Tyron arguing with what sounded like a creditor, so it's entirely possible we were threatened and I just never knew." She bared her fangs. "Just you wait until he gets home. I am absolutely going to *murder* him!"

Lakin and I exchanged a look, and I had a feeling he was going to send one of his deputies around to make sure Myrna didn't follow through on her threat.

We didn't get much more out of Myrna after that, so we moved onto the rest of the interviews on our list. About half of the victims had family in Rowanville while the other half were within the state of Canalo but out of town, so Lakin made some phone calls while I hopped on my bike to pay a few house calls. The shifters in Rowanville I could handle – they didn't have the same level of prejudice against me that the Shiftertown residents did. One for one, we found out the same thing – all of the victims, or their families, had taken a loan from Sandin Federal Bank at some point within the year, and each of them had failed to make payments.

"Well," Lakin said after we'd finished exchanging reports. "The evidence seems pretty conclusive at this point. The investor has got to be someone with significant control at Sandin Federal Bank, and access to confidential files."

"No kidding." An image of Warin Danrian's fear-filled eyes flashed in my mind. "I think it's time we head back to Sandin Federal ourselves to find out what Mr. Danrian was hiding. I have a feeling he knows exactly who that damned investor is, and where we can find him."

$\mathcal{U}$nfortunately for us, someone had already arrived at Sandin Federal Bank by the time we got there – the Mages Guild. Several horse-drawn carriages were parked in the small lot outside the bank, their doors stamped with the Guild's Logo – a seven-pointed star with a different rune hovering above each point, and an ornate 'M' stamped in the center. Two Privacy Guard employees stood watch in front of the doors, dressed in their blue uniforms, their eyes narrowed on Lakin and me as we pulled into the parking lot. Their white-gloved hands rested on the hilts of their short swords, ready for trouble, and their backs were ramrod straight.

"Ugh," Lakin muttered as he pulled off his helmet. "I hate these guys."

I nodded my agreement. Privacy Guard was a nation-wide company that contracted guards out to companies and government agencies like the Mages Guild. Some of the guards were decent, but a lot of them were assholes, and I'd been at the receiving end of their swords on more than one occasion. I'd nearly been beaten to death by a group of them during my first night at Solantha Palace, back when I was still a prisoner rather than an apprentice. And though these guards weren't the same ones who'd attacked me, I couldn't help stiffening at the sight of them.

Get it together, Naya. These guards are the least of your problems.

"Let's go find out what the hell is going on," I said to Lakin, and strode up to the guards.

The two men instantly closed ranks, blocking the door. "Can I help you Miss?" the thickset blond with mud-colored eyes on the right asked.

"Yeah." I folded my arms across my chest. "You can let me through so I can talk to whoever from the Guild is in there."

"I'm sorry, but we can't let you pass. Mr. Garidano was very specific in his instructions not to let anyone through."

"That's the Secretary of Finance, isn't it?" Lakin asked.

"Yep." I held up my enforcer bracelet for the guards to see. "Gentlemen, I'm not here to make a withdrawal. Inspector Lakin and I are investigating a series of disappearances in connection with Sandin Federal. If something is going on, we need to find out what it is."

The second guard, a lean man with pale skin and black hair, shifted a little beneath the weight of my gaze. "The bank's been shut down for illegal finance practices. The Finance Secretary and his team are sweeping the place."

"Excellent. Even more reason for you to invite me in."

When the guards didn't move, Lakin stepped forward. "Come on, guys. Don't you know who you're talking to? This is Sunaya Baine, the Chief Mage's apprentice. Do you *really* want her to have to get the Chief Mage involved just because you won't let her through the doors?"

I gritted my teeth, not enjoying Lakin's tactic, but the guards exchanged a look and stepped aside. One of them unlocked the front door and held it open. "Right this way, Miss Baine."

I shot Lakin a look as we stepped inside. "I don't really like to name drop, especially where the Chief Mage is concerned." The last thing I wanted to do was become even more reliant on him than I already was – I wanted people to respect me for who I was, and not for my connection to Iannis.

"Yeah, well I didn't want you to punch out the guards in broad daylight, so that was the best option." Lakin's eyes narrowed as we surveyed the space. There were apprentices everywhere, going through the teller drawers and bankers' desks and boxing up stacks and stacks of paperwork. "What are these guys doing here, anyway?"

"I went to talk to Fenris yesterday after we left the bank," I admitted quietly. "We figured out that the gold the bank was giving away was counterfeit, and Fenris said that he was going to deal with it. I guess this is what he meant by that." I gestured to the room.

"And you only thought to mention this *now*?"

I winced. "I kind of forgot about the counterfeit stuff after we watched all those shifters nearly kill each other yesterday," I admitted.

"Hmph." Lakin didn't sound any less annoyed. "Well I'm hoping they took all the employees into custody, or at least Danrian."

"Let's find out."

Lakin and I made our way over to Lena Moran, the Finance Secretary's assistant, who was standing in the center of the room and overseeing the apprentices. She wore a set of deep pink robes shot through with gold thread, and her light brown hair was piled atop her head in an elaborate tower of curls that made me want to snort with amusement. I'd seen her in the halls of Solantha Palace a couple times and she always looked like she was going to some kind of ball or event.

"Miss Baine!" Her hazel eyes lit as she saw me approaching.

"I'm happy to see you. I could use another apprentice to help us go through all of these boxes."

"Sorry Miss Moran, but I'm not here as an apprentice." I held up my bracelet. "I'm here as an enforcer. Where is the Finance Secretary?"

"Oh." She pressed her lips together in disappointment, then pointed behind her. "He's in the manager's office. I'm not sure he'll be happy to be interrupted though."

"Thanks." I brushed past her with Lakin in tow, making a beeline for Danrian's office.

Sure enough, the Finance Secretary was there, studying a huge, leather-bound ledger that had been laid out on the manager's desk. He glanced up at us in surprise as we walked in, his straight, jaw-length hair swinging around his thin, triangular face, and his dark eyes narrowed at the sight of me.

"Miss Baine." He straightened, his navy blue robes rippling with the movement. The golden seal of his office was stamped just below his left shoulder – a set of scales with a pile of gold on one end and a sheaf of wheat on the other. "Fenris told me you might show up."

"Great." I clasped my hands behind my back. "Then you must know the reason why I'm here."

"Presumably you're here to speak to Mr. Danrian." The Finance Secretary sighed. "Unfortunately he wasn't here when we raided the bank, much to my annoyance. The assistant manager said he'd run out to do an errand, and since he never came back I can only assume he realized what was happening and ran off. I sent a few guards to his house and they reported back that it looked like he'd packed up quickly and left. We're going to have to put out an alert for him."

"Shit." Lakin dragged a hand through his short, dirty-blond hair. His reddish-yellow eyes glimmered with anger as he glared at the Finance Secretary. "Couldn't you have staked the place out beforehand to make sure he'd be here? What kind of amateurs are you?"

The Finance Secretary stiffened, a dangerous look entering his dark eyes. "I would be very careful how you choose your words, Inspector. I'm a high-ranking member of the Guild, and you're a shifter, regardless of your status in the community. You do not have leave to speak to me in such a fashion."

Lakin clenched his jaw. "Nevertheless, you've cost us our only suspect with your reckless actions."

"Alright," I said, placing a hand on Lakin's shoulder. I couldn't believe that I was actually being the voice of reason here, but nobody else was volunteering. "There's no point in arguing about this. We've already fucked up, so the only thing we can do is try to fix it."

"And just how are we going to do that?" Lakin demanded.

I took in a deep breath. "We take this to the Enforcer's Guild."

LAKIN RECEIVED an emergency call from a shop in Shiftertown that was being robbed, so I headed up to the Enforcer's Guild on my own, hoping I'd find Annia there. I had to cool my heels in the visitor's chair by her desk, but eventually she walked in, her dark eyes sparking with anger as she caught sight of me.

"There you are!" She tossed a notebook onto her desk, then sat down in her chair. "Where the hell have you and Lakin been? I thought we were going to meet up at his house after the interviews were done, but you two never showed."

"Yeah, sorry about that." I winced. "We tried to call you, but we couldn't get through and we weren't sure how long you'd be on phone calls. All of our interviews led back to Sandin Federal and we wanted to jump on that as soon as possible."

Annia huffed. "Well, I guess we're all on the same page, at least. All my interviews pointed toward Sandin Federal as well. Did you grill the manager over there?"

"No." I let out a disgusted sigh. "The Mages Guild raided the place this morning, and the manager made himself scarce."

"Crap." Annia dragged a hand through her auburn hair. "Are there any clues as to where he might have bolted?"

"Not really. But I have a feeling that one of the the Shifter Royale staff might know." I drummed my fingers on the desk. "At this rate, the only thing we can do is shut down the Royale. I was hoping that you could come with me to talk to Captain Galling, so we could both convince him to get off his butt and send out a task force."

"Sure. I think he's in the house right now. Let's go."

Captain Galling's office was located on the top floor of the Enforcer's Guild building, along with the offices of his deputy and a few administrative workers. His was a corner office, with large windows looking directly out onto the street, and shelves full of books and weapons lining the walls. A large desk and a file cabinet took up half of the space, and there was a small cot in the corner which he supposedly used if he had to work late and didn't feel like going home. If he ever had used the thing, it was a relic of a bygone time, back when the Captain actually ran the Enforcer's Guild with a firm grip.

The man sitting behind the desk still looked commanding enough, with a large, strong build, close-cropped salt and pepper hair and beard, and hard, blue-black eyes. But his face and belly had softened from years of being off the streets, and I had a feeling that deep down inside, the Captain was just tired. He was in his late fifties, after all, and in human years that was significant. Also, from what I understood his wife was not in good health, and required his time and attention.

Still, that was no excuse for the way the Enforcer's Guild had been run for the past couple of years. And though I knew Captain Galling was cracking down on his enforcers more, mostly as a result of the Chief Mage's intervention, he wasn't doing enough, and probably wouldn't be until he started using that cot again.

"Baine, Melcott." Captain Galling lifted his head from his typewriter at the sound of my knock. "What do you need? I'm a little busy here."

"We're here to request a task force," Annia said, pushing her way past me and into the room.

"A task force?" Captain Galling's brow furrowed, and he pushed his typewriter aside. "What the hell for?"

"We've been assisting Inspector Lakin with investigating Sillara Tarenan's death," I told him. "We found out that she was investigating a series of shifter kidnappings, and traced the kidnappings to an underground fight club called the Shifter Royale." I explained the Royale to Galling, that Annia and I had attended one just the other night and we'd watched a number of drugged-out shifters pitted against each other in bloody fights.

"The manager of Sandin Federal disappeared today when Inspector Lakin and I went to question him," I said. "I have a feeling he knows who's behind this, and the only way to find him is via the Shifter Royale."

"Which needs to be shut down anyway," Annia insisted. "The operation definitely falls into enforcer territory, as it involves humans and shifters."

"And possibly mages," I added.

"Mages?" Galling's eyebrows shot up. "How do you know this?"

"At the end of each fight, the humans shoot the shifters with some kind of dart that not only knocks them unconscious, but forces them to change." The very memory of watching those shifters change while knocked out made me scowl.

"There's no way it was some herb or drug that did that. I'm convinced there was magic involved. Oh, and before I forget... two of the staff who were handling the shifters were also enforcers."

"What!" Captain Galling jumped out of his chair. "Who?"

"Brin Maxon and Nila Romana." I folded my arms across my chest. "Annia can confirm."

"I talked to them myself after the Royale was over," Annia said. "They were the ones who told me that the shifters participating in the fights were being forced into indentured servitude to pay off debts."

"This is unbelievable," Captain Galling growled, his tanned cheeks turning a dark, ugly red. Scowling, he snatched up his phone, then dialed Foreman Vance, the enforcer who was in charge of the Main Crew. "Vance? Are Maxon and Romana in the house today?" There was a pause. "Good. Send them up here. Yes, *now*."

A tense silence filled the room as we waited for Brin and Nila to arrive. The tick in Captain Galling's jaw told me that somebody was about to get an ass-kicking, and I smiled inwardly at the thought that Brin and Nila would finally be getting their comeuppance. It was about damned time. With the Mages Guild scrutinizing him more closely, Captain Galling was under pressure to clean up the Enforcer's Guild, and he wouldn't be able to tolerate Brin and Nila's actions.

The two came in about five minutes later, confusion stamped across their faces. Brin's eyes narrowed at the sight of Annia and I sitting there, and Nila's went curiously blank. I wondered if they knew what was about to happen.

"What can we do for you, Captain?" Nila asked, her voice slightly breathy as she stepped forward. She was wearing a long-sleeved leather corset top that pushed her boobs up front and center, and I had no doubt she was hoping to distract Captain

Galling with them. "Foreman Vance said you needed us urgently."

"Don't play dumb with me, Romana," Captain Galling snapped. His dark eyes did indeed fix on her cleavage, but only for a split second – he was too angry to be swayed by a nice rack, it would seem. "These two are telling me you're moonlighting for a company that runs an illegal fighting ring called the Shifter Royale, and that they *both* saw you there last night."

Surprise flashed in Brin and Nila's eyes as they glanced at me, and I knew they were wondering how we could have seen them if they hadn't seen us. But they couldn't very well point that out without incriminating themselves, so I simply folded my arms across my chest and smiled smugly at them.

"Sir, this is ridiculous," Brin said stiffly. "Nila and I don't have time to moonlight. We've got a pretty full docket, as part of the Main Crew."

"Exactly." Nila nodded decisively. "What reason would we have to moonlight?"

"Can either of you verify your whereabouts for yesterday evening?" Galling demanded.

"Sure. We were at Nila's apartment last night." Brin tossed an arm over Nila's shoulder and pulled her close. "As we are most nights."

Captain Galling rolled his eyes. "From someone *other* than yourselves?"

Another tense silence filled the room, which Annia broke. "Say, Brin, I notice you've got a bandage on your arm. What happened?"

"Sliced it in a sword fight," Brin growled.

"Oh yeah?" Faster than a speeding steambike, I jumped up and yanked Brin forward by the arm. He yelped as I closed my arm around the wound, and I grabbed one end of the gauze and ripped it off before he could retaliate. "Oh, would you look at that. These look like bite marks! From a tiger shifter, perhaps?" I gave him a big smile.

"Get off me!" Brin swung for my head, but I ducked, then twisted him around by the arm and slammed him face-first against the wall.

"It's about time I get the chance to arrest you," I snarled in his ear, pulling a pair of restraints from one of my pouches and slapping them on his wrists. "Unless you have an objection, Captain Galling."

"No, I don't."

"What?" Nila shrieked, her heart-shaped face purpling. "You can't arrest Brin! You don't have any real evidence!"

"I'm afraid the word of two enforcers, plus the fact that Brin just lied about his wound, is more than enough," Captain Galling said darkly as Annia cuffed Nila as well. He picked up the phone and called his deputy as she struggled against the restraints, but it was no use – Annia had her in a firm grip. A couple of minutes later, the Deputy Captain arrived with two other enforcers to take Brin and Nila away.

My eyes narrowed as I studied the new Deputy – he was a step-up from Garius Talcon, his predecessor, who'd sexually harassed me, beaten me, and attempted to rape me a few months ago. Unlike Talcon, who was fat, thuggish and leery, the new deputy was clean cut and trim, with a square face and steady blue eyes that swept over us all as he entered the room. Handsome but militant was the first impression I got – a far cry from Talcon's leers and waggling eyebrows.

Of course, looks could be deceiving – this guy could be just as depraved as Talcon. But I was really hoping he wasn't.

"Captain Galling." He inclined his head. "You want these two brought below for the night?" he asked, referring to the basement jail cells.

"Yes. We're holding them until further notice."

"You bitch!" Nila spat in Annia's face, her eyes wild. "I won't let you get away with this!"

"No, *you're* the ones who won't get away with this," Annia snarled, wiping flecks of spittle from her cheek as she jumped to her feet. I was on my feet as well, my fists clenched at my sides – I wanted to deck Nila, just this once, but I knew that wasn't going to win me any favors from Galling.

"You're done fucking with the lives of innocent shifters, Nila," I growled instead. "In fact, if I have it my way, you're done *period*."

"Pah!" Brin actually had the audacity to spit on my boot. "You shifters are all just mangy animals anyway." He began to struggle as the other enforcers pulled him from the room. "You're rabid beasts that need to be leashed for your own good!"

His shouts continued to echo from down the hall, and I glared at him as I watched him go. I was breathing hard from the effort of holding myself back from chasing him down the hall and beating him into a pulp. Because Brin thought humans were better than shifters, he was justified in drugging and kidnapping them and forcing them to kill each other? If anyone deserved that kind of fate, it was him.

"So," Captain Galling said, returning my attention to him. "You say you need a task force? When?"

"I'm not sure yet," Annia admitted. "We don't know when the next Royale is. But I have a feeling it'll be in the next few days, and with a bit of snooping around I should be able to find out when. I'll head over to Turain this afternoon."

"No." I shook my head vehemently. "You've already been there twice. It's going to look pretty suspicious if you're snooping around a third time. I'll go myself, in a different disguise."

"Are you sure?" Annia demanded. "You won't have any trouble with the smoke?"

"I'll dig up a charm from somewhere to help me deal with it. Trust me, Annia, it's better this way."

"Alright." Captain Galling pinned me with his hard stare. "You're certain that no one suspected anything after the magic stunt you pulled?"

"Not that I know of." I shrugged, the idea making me a little uneasy. "Nobody tried to stop or question us."

"Fine. But you'd better be right, Baine, because if you send us walking into an ambush I'll have your hide, Chief Mage's apprentice or not."

16

I tried to get out of my duties at the Mages Guild that afternoon so I could go to Turain, but the Chief Mage wasn't available, and Director Chen wasn't having it, so I was forced to spend the rest of the afternoon doing grunt work as usual. Dragging my feet down the hall on my way to the Secretary of Agricultural Magic's office, I was turning over an idea in my mind about how to convince him to let me out early when the Finance Secretary walked out of a room.

"Oh, Miss Baine." His eyes narrowed thoughtfully as he caught sight of me. "Where are you headed to?"

"Department of Agricultural Magic," I said, pointing down the hall. "Why?"

"Oh, well never mind Soren," the Finance Secretary said impatiently, referring to the Secretary of Agricultural magic by name. "This is more important than sending out letters to farmers. Come along." He waved me into the room he'd just come from.

"What exactly am I helping you with?" I asked warily as I entered the room. It was a large clerks' office, with rows of beige metal file cabinets lining the walls, and a number of desks arranged throughout the space, all covered with stacks of paper and ledgers. Many of the people sitting at the desks and going through these records were apprentices, but a few of them, to my surprise, were humans.

"The Mages Guild does employ human accountants to help me keep up with the regular work," the Finance Secretary said, correctly interpreting the question in my gaze. "The apprentices are all well and good, but I need some regular trained members on my staff, and there aren't very many mages who are willing to put aside spellcraft to work on numbers."

"Huh. I guess that makes sense." I knew *I* definitely wouldn't want to volunteer for the job.

I followed the Finance Secretary into his office, which was in a smaller, separate room that featured a large glass window enabling the Finance Secretary to observe the others in his department. Other than that, though, his own office was much the same as the outside room – lots of file cabinets, stacks of leather-covered dispatch boxes, and shelves filled with ledgers. There was a tiny golden set of scales on his desk that I assumed was meant to be used as a paperweight, and a small potted tree with a braided trunk that I recognized as a money tree.

"Does that thing really give you financial good luck?" I asked as I sat down in one of his visitor's chairs.

To my surprise, the Finance Secretary's lips quirked briefly as he eyed the plant. "No, but it's a gift from my wife, so I care for it all the same."

The small insight into his personal life reminded me that beneath their stony facades, mages were people too. I wondered if they were just as stiff and formal amongst their families in the privacy of their own homes, or if they showed more warmth. I'd glimpsed warmth in Iannis enough times to know that I couldn't discount the possibility.

The Finance Secretary's smile disappeared almost as quickly

as it had come, and he reached into a drawer behind his desk and pulled out a thick, leather-bound book. I recognized it as the ledger he'd been studying back in Danrian's office at Sandin Federal Bank.

"I found this ledger in a wall safe hidden behind a painting in the bank manager's office," the Finance Secretary said tersely, flipping it open. "I thought you might want to know about it."

"Oh yeah?" I leaned forward to study the contents, and had to squint my eyes to read the tiny, cramped script. But as I scanned the names and the numbers written in the columns, realization began to dawn on me as I recognized several of them from Sillara's list.

"These are all names of shifters who've taken loans from Sandin Federal Bank."

"Indeed. But it isn't just a record of those who've taken loans at the local branch, I don't think." The Finance Secretary tapped his fingers against the heavily inked paper. "These are specifically the names of shifters who haven't been keeping up with their payments, and lists the loan amount, the number of payments missed, and the number of times they've been contacted." The Finance Director pressed his lips together. "I've cross-checked some of these names in the records we confiscated, and a good number aren't customers of the local branch."

I frowned. "Then what are they doing in the ledger?"

"I'm not certain, but most likely these people are residents of different cities in Canalo, and will have taken out their loans at different branches all over the state."

I mulled this over for a moment, and my eyes widened as I realized the implications. "So Danrian wasn't just following orders like a good little manager. He's one of the main players involved!"

"It would seem so." The Finance Secretary scowled. "I've sent out telegrams to the Finance Directors of the other Guilds to have them look into the branches in their respective states, and also to the Federation's Finance Secretary as he'll need to shut down the corporate headquarters. I imagine whoever is behind this has a representative in each state, to ensure the operation is running smoothly. It stands to reason Mr. Danrian would be the representative for all of Canalo, especially since he resides here in the capital city."

"Right." I narrowed my eyes at the Finance Secretary. "Why exactly are you telling me all of this?"

His dark eyebrows winged up. "Because this is your investigation, of course, and it is pertinent information."

"True, but it's not my experience that mages are so helpful to shifters." Even now that I was an apprentice, when I had to go to another department for something, the mages there were always reluctant to engage with me.

"Ah, I see." Another smile tugged at the corner of his mouth. "You are wondering why I am deigning to help you even though you are a hybrid and therefore not worthy of my time and attention."

Anger began to simmer in my gut at the familiar supercilious tone in his voice. "Yeah, that sounds about right."

The Finance Secretary sighed. "Most of the mages around here feel that you should be given as little attention as possible, much in the way you ignore a spoiled child's tantrums until he eventually ceases to wail and the problem resolves itself. But I've been watching you, and it's apparent to me that you not only aren't going anywhere, but that you have influence with the Chief Mage. So rather than try to hinder you, I'm offering my assistance in the hopes that you'll remember me later on when I need a favor."

"A favor?" My own eyebrows jumped. "What kind of favor could you possibly want from me?"

The Finance Secretary shrugged. "I have ambitions just like

anyone else," he said. "Politically you may someday prove to be an asset. I am willing to help you along your way, and when the time comes I expect you'll remember my show of support."

I snorted. "I think you'd have a better chance of getting me to wear mage's robes than you would of getting me involved in politics."

"Perhaps, but you have a long life ahead of you, and you are only just at the beginning." The Finance Director pressed the tips of his fingers together and regarded me from over the tops of his short, manicured nails. "I've learned to trust my instincts, Miss Baine, and mine are telling me that you will at some point become a force to be reckoned with."

"Well thanks, I think." Pride swelled in my chest at that, and I forced it down before it inflated my head. "Is there anything else?"

"Yes." He closed the book. "I would like for you to help the other apprentices continue to go through the files. We need to get all of the information together to turn over to the legal department so they can begin prosecuting, and since I am one of the delegates accompanying Lord Iannis to the Convention I am extremely pressed for time. As it is, I am going to have to delay my departure because of this bank fiasco and miss my berth on the official airship."

I groaned. Great. More paperwork.

By the time I left the Finance Department, my eyes felt like they were bleeding and my head was so full of numbers I thought it was going to explode. My neck and shoulders ached from hunching over a desk all afternoon, and I really, *really* wanted to go down to Comenius's shop and beg him for one of his soothing tea blends. And maybe a shoulder rub.

But I didn't have time to hang out with Comenius, much as I would have liked to. I needed to head down to Turain and find out when the next Shifter Royale was taking place.

Just as I was about to enter the Guild's lobby, I spotted the Chief Mage, his cobalt blue robes rippling as he strode into the lobby. We locked eyes and stopped at the same time, Iannis in the center of the lobby while I hovered just inside the hallway.

"Miss Baine." The Chief Mage inclined his head. "I was just coming to look for you. You never showed up for your lesson."

"Huh?" Alarm shocked me out of my foggy state, and I pushed back the sleeve of my jacket to check the time. Eight fifteen. Over an hour late. "Crap. I'm sorry." I looked up to meet the Chief Mage's stern gaze. "I was helping the Finance Secretary sort through all the records he seized from Sandin Federal Bank this afternoon. I guess I lost track of time." Well that, and I'd completely forgotten we were scheduled to have a lesson tonight.

"Ah, yes." The Chief Mage's frown lightened. "I'm glad you finally investigated the bank. It would seem there was good reason to look into it."

"Yeah." I thought about telling him about the rest of the investigation, but I held back. I really didn't need Iannis's help with this, and he was so busy as it was. "Umm, so can I get some food before we start? I haven't eaten since noon."

"No need. I had dinner in my quarters with Fenris, and the cook brought more than enough food. If the leftovers aren't still there, I'll simply order more for you." He turned and headed back out of the lobby, clearly expecting me to follow.

"Hang on," I said, hustling to keep up with his long-legged stride. "We're not going to the training room?"

"No. We won't be needing it for what I have planned tonight."

Warmth blossomed in my cheeks as Iannis confirmed what

I'd suspected – he was taking me to his personal quarters. The last time I'd been there, the Chief Mage had briefly seen me naked, and we'd also fought about the idea of him making me his apprentice. I still remember the way my body had tingled as he'd pushed me up against the wall and pinned me with his violet eyes, and I remembered how they'd blazed. I hadn't been sure whether or not he was going to kill me or kiss me at the time, and the idea of being alone in that room with him again made my heart beat a little faster than it should have.

Then again that room was also the same place where the Chief Mage had unlocked the seal my father had placed on my magic, giving me control over my powers for the first time in my life. So there were good memories of that room too.

Despite being located on the far end of the West Wing, it didn't take very long for us to reach Iannis's quarters. I watched as he placed a hand on the brass knob and muttered an incantation, and the knob glowed briefly before the lock clicked open. I memorized the Words he'd used – I wanted to try that out for myself when I got home. With the way my life was going right now, it was probably a good idea to spell my locks so that nobody would try to ambush me in my own apartment.

I followed Iannis in through the open door, my eyes taking in the spacious, yet cozy sitting room. It was decorated in the Chief Mage's colors, the blue upholstery on the heavy, dark wood furniture and the matching curtains framing the large bay window embroidered with gold thread. The wall to my left was lined with bookshelves, and a large bay window on the right offered a wonderful view of the Firegate Bridge stretching across Solantha Bay. The couches were grouped around a marble fireplace, which lay dark and silent –no fire was needed at this time of year.

"Help yourself," Iannis said, gesturing to a table by the bay window where the remnants of a meal were laid out – half a platter of ribs, a partially empty bowl of roasted carrots and sweet potatoes, and some salad. "I'll return shortly."

I watched as he disappeared through a door on the far side of the room, then sat down and helped myself to the food. As I chewed on rib meat, which was cold but tasty, I stared out the window at the Firegate Bridge. I should have already been across it and halfway to Turain by now, but I had a feeling I wasn't going to have time to make the trip tonight. I would have to do it in the morning.

Once I polished off the food, I stood up and crossed to the other side of the room, perusing the books that lined the shelves. Many of the titles were in foreign languages, some of them even written in strange runes rather than letters, and I wondered just how many languages Iannis knew. I'd never asked his age, but I always assumed he'd lived several centuries already, which was plenty of time to amass quite a few languages. It made me wonder just how much knowledge I would have when I got that old.

If I got that old.

The door opened behind me, and I turned around to see Iannis clutching two gold chains in one of his fists. Small, white tanzarite stones swung from the ends of the chains, their fire catching the light, and I blinked, curious.

"What are those for?" I asked as Iannis closed the door behind him.

"Come sit down and you'll see."

I joined him on the couch, sitting as close to the armrest as possible. Even so, our knees nearly touched, and my pulse jumped as his masculine scent invaded my space.

"Tonight," Iannis said, holding out one of the necklaces to me, "you are going to learn how to make a charm."

"A charm?" I echoed, taking the piece of jewelry from him. I was careful not to let his fingers touch mine, but even so, my cheeks warmed at the idea of accepting something so beautiful from him. White tanzarite was one of my favorite gemstones; they were pure and full of fire. If I'd been the type of girl to buy myself jewelry I would have a whole collection of them.

But I doubted Iannis knew that, or that he'd chosen the stones based off what he thought my preference would be.

"Yes. Usually apprentices already know the basics of charm-casting; mage children are taught from an early age how to make simple ones." Iannis looked wryly down at the stone in my hand. "The ones we are going to make tonight are not simple, but with my help I'm certain you'll do fine."

"Cool." I glanced down at the chain in my hand, and noticed that it was more masculine, the links thicker and larger, than the one the Chief Mage had. "Umm, so what are we making, exactly?"

"We're making a set of *serapha* charms." Iannis paused for a moment, and he seemed to be watching my face for a reaction. When I only stared at him blankly, he continued. "These are worn by two different people, and can be used to locate the other at any given time. I thought it would be a good alternative to the tracking spell I placed on you, as you can take this off whenever you feel you must have privacy – though nobody else can take it off for you. And you can also use it to track me down, should you have need of me."

"Oh." Touched, I stroked the tiny round stone, which was about the size of my pinky nail. "You don't need to go through all this trouble. I'd already forgotten about the tracking spell."

Iannis shrugged. "Fenris suggested it. I think it's a good idea, and also an excellent opportunity to teach you about charm-casting."

"Okay." I wasn't about to argue, especially since this would allow me to locate the Chief Mage whenever I wanted, eliminating the need to rely on others to tell me where he was. "So what do we do?"

Iannis unclasped the necklace, then fastened it around his own neck. He positioned the stone so that it sat directly over his heart, then placed his hand over it and held it there.

"*Serapha* charms require you to imbue them with a small piece of your life force... your soul, if you will. You simply place the necklace over your head like I have done, and then repeat the incantation I'm about to use."

"Alright." A little shiver rippled down my spine at the idea of giving up a piece of my soul for this, but as I looked down at the tiny stone I figured it was probably a very small piece. Mimicking Iannis, I fastened the chain around my neck, then placed the stone over my heart.

Iannis closed his eyes, then spoke the Words. I watched his brow furrow, as if in pain or discomfort, and the scent of magic thickened in the air. Blue-white spilled out through the cracks between his fingers, and I flinched at the brightness, but it faded quickly, as did the burnt-sugar scent in the air.

When Iannis lifted his hand from the stone, I noticed it was glowing brightly, but the brilliance was self-contained.

"It will fade after a little while," Iannis explained, correctly interpreting my gaze. "Once the spell settles, it will only activate again when you have need of the charm. Now, you try it."

I took a deep breath in through my nostrils to steady my nerves, then repeated the incantation. I felt a pinch deep inside me, in a place I'd never even felt before, followed by a burning sensation, and I stifled a yelp of surprise. But it was over before I knew it, and when I opened my eyes I could see my own stone glowing. It felt hot beneath my fingers, as if there wasn't just light, but fire in its depths.

"Very good." Iannis nodded, a pleased expression on his

face, and then he ducked his head so he could remove the necklace. "And now we exchange necklaces."

I did as he asked, trading my necklace for his, and it occurred to me that this was rather intimate, the idea of trading a piece of one's soul for a piece of someone else's. But I supposed since we were master and apprentice that wasn't so strange – Roanas and I had shared a very close bond. I wondered if Iannis and I would ever become close in that way, if the sexual tension between us would ever fade, or if it would always keep us from truly relaxing around each other so we could bond the way a mentor and his student should.

As I placed Iannis's necklace around my neck, the stone's glow gradually faded until it appeared nothing more than an ordinary gemstone. But I could still feel a faint warmth emanating from the stone as it rested against my chest.

"Excellent." Iannis's eyes were surprisingly soft as he regarded me. "Now we're properly linked."

"Seems so." I looked down at the pendant again. "So how exactly do I use this thing?"

"It's a simple enough charm. You speak my name while holding the pendant, and you'll get an instant sense of where I am. Go on, try it."

"Okay." I curled my fingers around the necklace, making sure that the pendant was touching my palm. "Iannis ar'Sannin."

Instantly, a sense of intuition activated inside me, and it was as if a map unfolded in my mind's eye, revealing a pulsing dot where Solantha Palace was. I couldn't actually *see* the map though, nor the pulsing dot; it was more like I could sense it, and I had the idea that if I wasn't actually at the Palace, something inside me would tug me towards Iannis's location, even though I wouldn't actually know that's the location I was headed.

I let go of the pendant, and the feeling faded away. "Whoa. That was weird."

Iannis cracked a smile. "But it works, does it not?"

"It sure does." I grinned. "Does this mean you're going to remove the tracking spell now?"

"It does."

He scooted closer, and I jumped a little as he took my hands in his. Warmth flowed through me from his hands to mine, pooling in my lower belly, and suddenly I was filled with *want*. Our gazes locked, and his iridescent violet eyes burned into mine for just a moment.

"This will only take a second."

He spoke another short incantation, and a wave of magical energy rushed across my skin, sending tingles from my head to my toes. And then he dropped my hands, and it was over.

"Unfortunately I've no time left to teach you more since we started so late," he said, his tone tinged with regret. "You should be on your way now."

"Wait!" The word burst from my lips as Iannis began to stand. I had a feeling there was something I was supposed to be telling him, something important, but my brain was too overwhelmed to tell me what. Instinctively I reached out and grabbed his wrist, then bit back a gasp as heat lightning arced between us.

"Yes?" Iannis's eyes flared, but not with anger, and I *knew* that he felt it too. This strange connection we had, whatever it was, it was *real*. And as he stood above me, I had a feeling that we were both standing on opposite ends of a canyon, and that Iannis was just waiting for the right word from me to jump across it to the other side.

But the words, whatever they had been, dried on my tongue, and I swallowed. "Thank you," I said quietly, looking away. I jumped to my feet, releasing his hand as I did so. "I have to go now. Goodnight."

And I fled the room, leaving my pride somewhere between the Chief Mage's couch cushions.

17

*T*t was after nine o'clock by the time I finally made it out of the Palace, too late for me to be driving up to Turain now, so I reluctantly decided to postpone my trip until tomorrow. A little lost, I toyed with the idea of seeking out Comenius or Noria, but at this hour of the night I figured they'd be with their lovers, so I went on home instead.

After trying out the spell I'd seen Iannis use on my own doorknob – yes, it *did* work! – I traded in my leather pants and jacket for a pair of cotton shorts and a tank top, then climbed into bed with the *Residah*, hoping the thick leather tome would lull me to sleep.

As I propped the book up on my thighs, it seemed to open of its own accord, the pages flipping until they finally settled on a chapter regarding self-control. My eyebrow arched, and I wondered if whichever god was watching from above was trying to send me a message. In any case, I figured it was as good a place as any to start, so I began reading.

Self-control is possibly the most important quality a mage must cultivate. In order to safely practice magic, a mage must have achieved mastery over every aspect of their existence – mind, body

and soul. Magic is controlled by thought and intention, thus it is neces-
sary to have a firm grip one one's emotions before casting even the
most minor spell. To do otherwise could have catastrophic results.

I pursed my lips as I thought about that. I'd always made fun
of mages for being so stoic, but if they were taught from an early
age that controlling their emotions was necessary to mastering
magic, I supposed it only made sense that they were raised that
way. And though I'd seen Iannis use his magic while angry a
time or two, he'd never done so while performing any kind of
major spell, and even when he'd been angry he'd somehow
seemed in control. I knew that if I had the kind of power he did
and I lashed out with the full force of my anger, I would cause
all kinds of damage. Maybe he was right to place limits on my
magic until I was ready to handle more.

I was about to dive back into the book when a loud knock at
the door startled me. Jerking my head up, I strained my ears for
any sign that there might be trouble – visitors were a rarity.

"I don't think she's home." I blinked at the sound of Comenius's voice.

"Of *course* she is home." A woman's richly accented voice
floated through the crack beneath the doorway as I quickly
shrugged on a robe and hurried into the living room. "You said
the steambike parked at the curb belonged to her, did you not?
And the lights are on. She must be here."

"Well yes, but that doesn't mean she's –"

"Hey!" I threw open the door, a smile tugging at my lips at
the thought of seeing a friendly face. Sure enough, Comenius
was standing in the hall, dressed in one of his dark green tunics,
and on his arm was his new girlfriend, Elania. "Wasn't expecting
any visitors."

"I can see that," Elania said, her throaty accent tinged with
amusement. Her dark gaze swept over me, and as I took in her
flawless pale skin, her perfectly curled, inky black hair, and

the deep red velvet dress that hugged her curves, a wave of self-consciousness swept through me. But if she was unimpressed with my outfit, or lack thereof, she didn't show it outwardly, so I tried to push the feeling aside and smiled at her.

"Sorry, Naya." Comenius scratched the back of his head, looking vaguely embarrassed. "I can see that you were in bed, and we didn't mean to disturb you –"

"Yes we did," Elania said firmly, but kindly, squeezing Comenius's arm. "My *iubito* has been fretting about you for the past few days, ever since he heard about your involvement with the terrorist attack on the bridge, to the point that it's been affecting our time together. So I brought him over here to see you, so he can assure himself you are alive and well."

"Oh." Guilt and shame burned at my cheeks – I should have considered the possibility that like Annia, Comenius would have found out about my involvement with the bridge, and that he would have worried about me. "I'm sorry, Com. I've just been so distracted these last couple of days. I should have thought to drop by. Please, come in."

I stepped back to let them in, and Elania's bourbon-vanilla scent drifted past me, making my nose twitch. I'd seen her around once or twice at Witches End; she was a witch who specialized in potions, as in rather than making you a good luck charm, she'd whip up a lucky elixir for you instead. From what I heard she also did the occasional hex under the table, but since those were illegal I'm sure she'd deny it if someone like me came around her shop asking for one.

"I will make tea," Elania announced as I shut the door. "You do have tea, correct?"

"Umm, yeah. I think I've got some chai in one of the cupboards, and there's milk in the fridge." I hurried over to the kitchen to grab the ingredients.

"Chai will do," Elania decided, pulling out a small teapot from one of my cupboards and filling it with water.

"No time to go food shopping?" Comenius asked casually as he caught a glimpse of the inside of my empty fridge.

I sighed, setting the milk on the counter. "You could say that. Between working at the Mages Guild and helping Lakin with this case, I barely have time to breathe."

"Are you talking about those disappearances we were looking into the last time you came to visit?" Comenius asked, joining me in the living room. I settled myself onto my recliner, tucking my legs beneath me, while he took the couch.

"Yeah. It turns out that all of them are being forced into indentured servitude in order to pay off debts." I gave him a brief overview of the Shifter Royale and all that we'd discovered, and also told him that my cousin's daughter, Mika, had been taken because I'd refused to let go of the investigation.

"Oh, Naya." Comenius's voice was full of sympathy. "I'm so sorry to hear about Mika. I know you're not close with your family, but I'm sure it's not been easy."

"I try not to think about it too much." I let out a gusty sigh. "Mainly I've just been focusing on how to catch the bastard responsible. I'm going to find out when the next Shifter Royale is, and then Annia and I are going to take a task force in there and bust open the whole operation."

"Well I hope you'll keep me updated on this, and let me know if I can be of any help."

Elania glided over with the tea pot and three empty mugs, all of which she balanced on a metal baking sheet that she'd repurposed as a tea tray. She didn't seem at all bothered by my lack of a traditional tea service, but I suddenly was, though I'd never really thought about it before. All of my cutlery and dishes were mismatched; I'd never seen the point in getting a set as I didn't entertain guests. But my circle of friends and acquaintances was expanding, and I had a feeling I would need to adjust accordingly.

"Thank you," I told her, leaning forward to take a cup of steaming chai. As I did so, the chain around my neck swung forward, revealing the white stone dangling from the end.

Elania's eyes gleamed as she caught sight of the jewel. "That's a very pretty necklace," she commented, settling onto the couch next to Comenius with her own cup of tea in hand. "It has power of some kind, does it not?"

"Yes." I touched the tanzarite pendant, feeling a little self-conscious about it. I had a feeling it wasn't something I was supposed to be wearing openly, but I didn't think to keep it hidden once I'd tucked myself into bed. "It's called a *serapha* charm."

"A *serapha* charm!" Comenius exclaimed, his tea sloshing around in his cup as he sat up straight. "Who in the world did you exchange *serapha* charms with?"

"Umm, the Chief Mage." An uneasy feeling settled in my stomach at the alarm in Comenius's eyes. "I was pretty pissed when I found out that he'd put a tracking spell on me, so he offered this as a compromise. That way we can both find each other if there's any other trouble."

"I see." Comenius and Elania exchanged a look.

"What?" I demanded, not at all liking the feeling that I was being left out of the loop. "Why are you guys acting so weird? Did I do something wrong?" And how did they know I'd exchanged charms with someone, rather than simply been given one?

"No," Comenius said, turning back to me again. "It's just that *serapha* charms are usually exchanged between two mages who are getting married."

"To each other," Elania added helpfully, as if that wasn't clear.

I stared at them both, open-mouthed. "You...what...this is supposed to be a *wedding gift?*"

"Generally speaking," Comenius said. "I've heard of family members exchanging them before, usually siblings who need to be able to keep track of the other for whatever reason. But generally it's two lovers who are married or are to be married."

"Well the Chief Mage and I are master and apprentice," I declared, setting my teacup down. "That's a pretty close bond, almost like family, wouldn't you say?"

"I suppose," Elania said, though there was doubt in her voice. "It *is* generally frowned upon for a master and apprentice to have carnal relations."

"Exactly." I tried to ignore the way my heart sank at Elania's reminder. "This might be a little unconventional, but it's one of the only ways the Chief Mage can keep tabs on me if something happens, and with the way my life's going right now I can't say his concerns are unfounded."

"Well, that I agree with." Comenius frowned. "Are you sure you wouldn't like me to come with you to Turain tomorrow, Naya? I don't know that it's safe for you to go."

I waved a hand. "No, you've got a shop to run. Besides, I've already been up there twice and nothing happened. You know I can take care of myself. I haven't seen anything there yet that I can't handle with either my magic or my weapons."

"Alright," Comenius relented. "Just, be careful, won't you? It's only been two months since your last brush with death."

I smiled. "Don't worry. I'll be fine."

THE NEXT DAY, I stopped at a deli to grab a sandwich, then took off for the gambling den. As I rode my bike up the long, hilly road, I thought about simply investigating on my own to find out where the missing shifters were being held. If I could find Mika and the others before the next Royale was scheduled, maybe I could find a way to smuggle the captives out. After all, I was resourceful, and I had a decent amount of magic at my disposal, not to mention my weapons. Surely it was worth a shot?

The hot summer sun beat down from above as I rode into Turain, bathing my skin in a light sweat beneath my leather jacket. I parked my bike around the block from the Dirty Habit in an alley behind a row of shops, then reached for my magic so I could put on my illusion. I'd have to pick something different than the blonde bimbo, since she wouldn't show up here without Annia. If I thought I could fake Annia's confidence with gambling, I'd even pretend to be her.

But just as I was taking off my helmet, I heard a tiny *zip*, the sound of something flying through the air at top speed, and then a sharp pain burst into the side of my neck.

"Oww!" I grabbed at the dart that had lodged itself into my flesh. "What the fuck?"

A human dropped down from the rooftop, dressed in black with a scarf wrapped around his face despite the warm weather. My vision started to blur as the drug in the dart began to take effect, spreading icy-hot fire through my veins, but I heard the sneer in his voice as he approached.

"Sorry Miss Enforcer, but Mr. Danrian told us to watch out in case you ever came around here. Looks like you're not making it to your destination today."

"Fuck you." I grabbed one of the chakrams from my pouch and threw it at him, but my arms were growing shaky, and my throw flew wide. My assailant laughed as the chakram embedded itself in the brick wall ten feet from him, and I cursed as I dropped to my knees, my legs too rubbery to hold me any longer.

"*HELP!*" I cried out mentally, hoping, *praying* there was a shifter nearby who might hear my call. But there was no one, and I kicked myself for my foolish decision to come here without backup. Of *course* Danrian would have known I was looking for him. What was I thinking?

"Sweet dreams," my assailant said, toeing me with his booted foot, and I fell right over, through the ground and into the darkness.

18

The sensation of something pounding at my temples woke me, and it took me a second to realize that it was pain. Deep, throbbing pain, banging mercilessly at my skull. My mouth was dry as dust, my nerves were raw, and when I tried to move the pounding on my temples increased.

"Hello? Are you awake already?"

My eyes popped open at the sound of the voice, and as my vision focused, I saw a pair of orange eyes staring at me through a set of bars. No, two sets of bars, I realized as sharp panic bit into me. One set was from her cage, and the other one was from mine.

"I am." I rolled onto my side and looked around. We were in a dark chamber, the only source of light coming from a single bulb hanging from the ceiling. It gave enough light for me to see the rows and rows of cages, nearly all of them filled with shifters, and my heart grew cold as I realized there were probably seventy others in the room with us. *"Where am I?"*

"I don't know. None of us do. This is just where they keep us between fights."

"Great." I tried to struggle up into a sitting position, and that's

when I noticed the manacles around my wrists. Concentrating my attention on them, I tried to use fire to soften up the metal enough to break the restraints, but though I could feel the magic flowing just beneath my skin, it refused to manifest.

"No." The panic in my chest tripled, and I jerked the chain binding my wrists together in a futile attempt to break them. "No, no, no!"

"They bind us all that way." The tiger shifter lifted her own manacled wrists. Anger burned deep in her orange eyes as she stared at me. *"We're a lot easier to control in human form."*

"No shit," I muttered, staring down at my shackled wrists. The runes on these were exactly the same as the ones on the shackles the mages had used to bind my magic when I'd been arrested. There was absolutely zero chance that I would be able to use my magic to get out of here. But something brushed against my chest, and as I caught sight of a white jewel winking in the darkness, I remembered that I still wore the *serapha* pendant the Chief Mage had given me. Relief sang through me – he would be able to find out where I was.

But only if he thinks to look for you.

My heart sank at the realization. Iannis was leaving for the capital tomorrow – he likely wouldn't even notice I was missing. Someone else might, like Annia or Captain Galling, and they might try to alert the Chief Mage, but how long would that take? He'd be on the other side of the continent by then.

"Any idea how long I've been here?"

"Since this morning. I watched them bring you in." The tigress cocked her head. *"I'm surprised you're awake so soon. It usually takes a full twenty-four hours to recover from a full-strength injection of the serum."*

Huh. Well that was something. Maybe being a hybrid made me more resistant to some shifter-specific drugs. I could only hope that was the case, because I had a feeling they were going to dose me up again so they could toss me in the fighting ring. Otherwise they would have just killed me.

I patted down the length of my body as best I could with my shackled wrists, trying to determine whether or not my captors had left me with anything useful. But aside from the *serapha* charm, they'd stripped me of all my weapons and pouches. I wasn't too concerned about my chakrams or my crescent knives – when the Chief Mage had recovered them for me, he'd spelled them so that they would return to me if lost or stolen. But this was the first time I'd been separated from my weapons since then, so I had no idea how long it would take for them to make their way back.

Rather than worry about something I had no control over, I turned my attention towards something I did. *"Do you know if a young jaguar female was brought in here?"* I asked the tigress. *"Sometime in the last couple of days?"*

"I think I remember seeing someone like her being dragged in. She hasn't been taken out for any fights yet."

Relief swept through me, and I sat up, mentally calling out for her. *"Mika, can you hear me?"* I shouted, projecting my voice to everyone in the room. *"Mika, are you here?"*

There were a lot of grunts and grumbles from the other shifters, who were evidently not happy with me shouting in their heads. But a female voice spoke in my head, small and hesitant, but clear.

"Yes, I'm Mika. Who's calling for me?"

I nearly collapsed with relief. *"It's Sunaya. Sunaya Baine. I'm your mother's cousin."*

"Oh!" I felt her joy for just a moment, and then she recoiled. *"Wait. You're the illegitimate one that the Chieftain kicked out, aren't you? The one who turned out to be half-mage?"*

"Are we really going to focus on that right now?"

"My mother's said bad things about you, and that if I should ever cross paths with you to stay as far away as possible."

"Yeah, well your mother also sent me here to rescue you," I told her dryly. "So I think you can put the other mandate aside, for now."

"I guess you're right, Mika replied dubiously. "Although, how are you supposed to get us out of here if you're stuck in a cage yourself?"

"I'm still working on that one."

I mindspoke to Mika and the other shifters for a little while, trying to glean anything useful out of them, but I didn't learn much. Because the shifters here were drugged so often, their memories were fuzzy and they couldn't answer most of my questions. Even Mika, who hadn't been in any fights yet, had been given regular doses to keep her drowsy and relatively compliant.

With nothing constructive to do, I lay back down in my cell and catnapped, determined to conserve my strength. I would take the first opportunity I had to escape and hopefully free the others, but until then, with no food in my belly and no access to my magic, the only thing I could do was wait.

I wasn't certain how long I lay in the dark, but when the sound of a garage door opening woke me, I realized that I'd fallen asleep at some point. Sitting up, I watched about twenty men stride into the room through the open doorway. Beyond them, I could see a huge truck parked just outside, the back doors opened, and I knew they were here to take some of us to the Royale. My entire body stiffened as I caught sight of Warin Danrian, who was bringing up the rear.

"You bastard," I hissed as he sauntered up to me, looking awfully smug. "You won't get away with this."

"Oh, but I already have." Sneering, Danrian crouched down in front of my cage so he could meet me at eye level. Behind him, the other men were moving the cages out of the room, "You may have shut down the bank, but our operation extends far beyond Sandin Federal. I may not be able to continue the Shifter Royale in Canalo thanks to your antics, but believe you me, our plan is well underway. You may as well forget about being rescued by those mages you hang out with – soon they'll be too buried under their own troubles to spare you a thought."

"'Our' plan?" I spat. "So I was right – you're in league with the Benefactor, aren't you?"

Danrian's eyes narrowed. "So Petros Yantz did tell you about the Benefactor," he said. "I always knew his lips flapped a little too much."

"Is there a fucking roster somewhere listing out all the members of Club Benefactor, and do you all get together once a month for tea or something?" I demanded. "Because that would be really helpful."

Danrian laughed. "Even if there was, it wouldn't be much use to you after you're dead. Surely you must know you're going to fight tonight."

"How do you know I won't survive?" I sneered, refusing to show the fear that was pumping through my veins.

"Because you're going up against your beloved cousin, and I have no doubt that someone of your principles would rather die than kill a family member."

Cold horror spilled through my veins, and I turned my head just in time to see Mika's cage being hefted onto a forklift.

"NO!" I railed at the bars of the cage, slashing at Danrian's throat, but I couldn't reach far enough with the shackles binding my wrists. "You bastard, leave Mika out of this! Let her go!"

"I'm afraid not." Danrian stood up, and regarded me with his cold, dark eyes. "I warned you not to get involved and you didn't listen, so now you're about to pay the price. Boys, put her under."

One of the men beside him stepped forward, that tube-like instrument in his hand again, and I ducked my head to avoid the first dart. But the second one struck me in the shoulder, and my vision went hazy in a matter of seconds. The last thing I saw was the forklift approaching my cage, and then I was out.

I CAME awake with battle fever pounding through my veins, the urge to kill so strong that I lunged forward without even knowing whether or not there was an enemy in front of me to kill. My forehead smashed into the iron bars, and I snarled, falling back against the hard floor and clutching my head.

Fuck, that hurt!

The pain cleared my head a little, and I sat up into a crouch. The battle fever continued to sing through my veins, and I trembled with the effort of holding myself together long enough to take stock of my surroundings. Not that I really needed to – the bright lights jabbing at my brain and the fighting cage looming just thirty feet from me told me that I was at the Royale.

Gritting my teeth, I turned my head and scanned the other cages in search of Mika. She was only two cages down from me, gripping the bars and snarling like a madwoman, her eyes bloodshot and her fangs dripping saliva. The sight stirred my own bloodlust, and I growled, my beast wanting her blood.

Stop it. Mika is family.

"Ladies and Gentlemen!' the announcer cried, and I turned my head to watch him. "Thank you all for coming out tonight! For our first match, we have a very special treat – black panther vs. jaguar! In case you don't know, these two cats are actually the same species, so it's a matter of light versus dark rather than a battle between species. I hope you placed your bets accordingly!"

The crowd burst into excited whoops and yells, and I braced myself as I watched several of the humans stride purposefully toward my cage. I tried to attack them as they dragged me from my cell, but they were fast and well trained, and I was still weak from the drugs as well as lack of food – I hadn't eaten since that measly sandwich in the early morning, and it had to be past nightfall by now.

The humans shoved me up a set of stairs leading to the platform, and then through the doors. I waited for them to unbind my wrists, but they simply slammed the doors shut on me, and I watched in horror as they walked off.

How the fuck am I supposed to fight if I can't even get my hands free?

By Magorah, no wonder Danrian wasn't concerned about my odds. He'd set me up so that I couldn't defend myself even if I wanted to.

They tossed Mika into the ring next. I watched as she staggered in, my anxiety growing as I noticed her bloodshot eyes glowing with malevolence. Just what shit had they drugged us with? She snarled as soon as she caught sight of me, and a white glow enveloped her body as she began to change.

"No!" I cried. "Mika, it's Sunaya! You don't want to kill me!" My own battle fever was tempered by the icy fear flooding through my veins – if I rushed to attack Mika like this, there was no way I'd win, shackled in human form with my magic cut off from me. My sense of self-preservation was much stronger than the drug they'd pumped into my system.

But it was too late. She'd shifted, and her eyes blazed with battle fever as she crouched, tail whipping back and forth right before she pounced. I darted out of the way as she sailed through the air, and she went crashing into the silver-coated bars of the cage. She let out a pained yowl, and I winced as I caught the stench of burning hair and flesh. Hopefully the injury would slow her down a little.

Mika landed on her side, but she quickly rolled back onto

her feet, then flexed her powerful leg muscles before pouncing at me again. This time, I took a gamble and rushed forward, my arms outstretched to meet her halfway. Her jaws closed around the chain binding my manacles, and I forced them all the way down to her mandibles, pushing her back. She lost her footing for a moment, and when she finally yanked away, two of the links ripped free.

Yay. At least I could use my hands now.

Mika reared up on her hind legs and swiped at me with a paw, and I hissed as her claws raked across my upper arm, leaving deep gashes. I twisted away, darting to the other side of the ring, but I knew it was only a matter of time before she caught me with a fatal blow.

Just as Mika spun around to face me again, I felt something thump onto the ground next to my boot. I glanced down, and elation burst through me at the sight of my chakram pouch and crescent knives. Finally, they'd arrived! Thinking quickly, I snatched up the knives first, then rushed forward to meet Mika as she lunged for me again. This time I twisted to the right, letting her pass me, and I raked the blade along the side of her rib cage, making sure the cut was deep enough to cause significant damage without being fatal.

Mika let out an ear-splitting roar as she fell to the ground, and I winced sympathetically – I knew from experience how painful cuts from crescent knife blades could be. But I didn't have time to stand around – I only had a few moments before Mika's wound healed itself and she was back on her feet again. Whirling around, I snatched up the chakram pouch, then grabbed one and twirled it briefly around my index finger before flinging one toward the tops of the bars. It cut through the silver-coated bamboo with ease, and I tossed another one toward the bottom of the cage, slicing the bar off at both ends. It toppled outward, landing with a loud clatter on the concrete ground, and the crowd screamed as I jumped through the opening.

Several of the staff rushed toward me, but I used my chakrams to cut them off at the knees – literally. They screamed in pain as the circular blade bit into the flesh of their legs, severing clear through, but I didn't even give them a second glance – I was already sprinting for Danrian, who was racing for the hidden doorway I knew was located in the wall behind the shifter cages.

"Stop!" I shouted, twirling another chakram around my index finger. "Stop, or I'll cut your head off, I swear!"

Danrian froze, his eyes wide with fear and loathing as he eyed the spinning metal disk – I knew he had no doubt that I would follow through on my threat.

"How did you get those weapons in here!" he shouted as I advanced on him. "Those shackles are supposed to prevent you from using magic!" He pointed toward the restraints on my wrists, his finger trembling.

"Guess I've got a few tricks up my sleeve," I sneered, grabbing him. Cries and screams echoed off the walls along with the sounds of dozens of stampeding feet, and I knew the humans were all rushing for the exit behind us again. Regardless of what happened to Danrian tonight, the Shifter Royale was finished – nobody was coming back after two incidents like this.

I didn't have any cuffs of my own on me, so I turned Danrian around and slammed him face first against the wall, twisting one arm behind his back and pushing upward so that he was forced onto his toes. He cried out in pain, but I only pushed harder, the battle fever still surging within me redirected to a new purpose.

"Tell me who the Benefactor is. Now!"

"I can't do that!" He choked out. "The Benefactor will kill me for sure if I do!"

"If you don't tell me right now, *I'm* going to kill you!"

A set of fangs sank into the back of my calf, and I cried out as burning pain ripped through the muscle. Shocked, I twisted away, letting go of Danrian so I could confront my attacker. My blood dripped from Mika's fangs as she snarled and charged at me again, still crazed from the drugs. My leg was too weak for me to dodge, so I dropped to the ground and rolled to the side, then slashed at her again with my knives. I got her in the side again, and she roared as the wound from last time, which was not fully healed, split open again.

The battle fever pumping hard through my veins allowed me to spring to my feet, and I grabbed Danrian, who had been trying to sidle away, by the arm. "Come on. We've got to get out of here!" As much as I wanted to release the shifters from their cages now, I knew they would all just attack us – I needed to get us to safety and wait for the Enforcer's Guild to show up. They had to be on their way by now. They just had to.

"I'm afraid I'm not going anywhere with you, Miss Baine," Danrian said smugly as I spun him around. I caught the glint of three darts in his hand as he raised it in the air, and I tried to avoid them, but momentum was on his side. I cried out as the darts jabbed me in the side of the neck, then screamed in agony as the icy hot poison rushed through my veins, stronger and more painful than last time. Fear burst through me, followed by a healthy dose of disgust – I couldn't believe that I was about to die at the hands of a filthy human like him.

"That dose will definitely kill you if Mika doesn't." Danrian's voice sounded very far away as I sank to the ground. I looked up at him, and it was like I was staring at him from the bottom of a pool – his form wavered, too blurry for me to focus on properly. "You came close to winning, but not close enough. On behalf of the Benefactor, I give you my regards."

He disappeared then, and the last thing I saw was Mika's bloody fangs before everything went dark.

19

"Do you think she's ever going to wake up?"

My mind stirred at the familiar male voice, which sounded distant beyond the black, greasy fog that seemed to surround me. It took me a moment to put a name to the voice – Fenris.

Who was Fenris?

"Of course she's going to wake up. Do you doubt my healing abilities?" another voice snapped – and this one I recognized instantly; Iannis. My heart warmed at the edge in his voice – he must be concerned for me.

Why was he concerned for me?

"No, it's just that she was struck with *three* darts." Fenris's voice came again, and this time a picture of a wolf with coarse brown hair floated into my mind. Ah, yes. I remembered him now. "The amount of silver in them would have killed any full-blooded shifter."

"Sunaya is forged from stronger stuff. She will pull through."

Huh. He'd used my first name. I'd never heard him use my name before. I kind of liked the way it sounded when he said it –

kind of exotic with his musical accent. I wanted him to say it again.

"Are her eyelids flickering?" Fenris's voice turned urgent. "Iannis, I think she can hear us!"

Strong fingers wrapped around my hand, and their warmth drew my attention to how cold I was. I was half-frigid, half-numb, and I wondered whether my body was actually encased in a block of ice. But those warm fingers squeezed mine, and some of the ice retreated.

"Sunaya. Can you hear me?"

I cracked my eyelids open to see Iannis's face hovering above mine. Anxiety shimmered in his gorgeous violet eyes, and I was so happy to see those eyes again that I could have kissed him.

"Are we on a first name basis now?" I croaked.

Fury eclipsed the anxiety in Iannis's eyes, and his grip on my hand tightened painfully. "Certainly not. Being on a first-name basis would imply a level of trust we have clearly not achieved, or you would have clued me into the extreme danger of your investigation."

Guilt settled onto my chest, a heavy weight that made it hard to breathe. "I'm sorry," I muttered, lowering my eyes.

"Why didn't you tell me about the Shifter Royale, or about your plans to apprehend them? I could have provided assistance and possibly prevented this whole catastrophe."

"Iannis." Fenris's voice was low, but firm, and he gently pulled Iannis back, allowing me to see that he was sitting in the chair next to the Chief Mage. He smiled at me. "I think now might not be the best time to berate her. She's clearly very tired."

I smiled back at Fenris, thankful for his intervention, but I held fast to Iannis's hand, not wanting him to go before I explained myself. "I didn't... keep it from you because I... distrust you." Getting the words out was an effort, but I was determined. "I just knew you were so busy... and wanted to show you I could take care of this myself. I'm sorry."

Iannis sighed, his eyes searching mine as he leaned forward. "There is no need for you to apologize. I can see that you were simply trying to ease my workload, as foolish as it was for you to leave me out of this. In the future, though, I expect you to fill me in on investigations that have far-reaching ramifications such as this one."

"I guess I can do that."

His lips twitched into a smile as he brushed a curl of hair back from my face. "When I return from my trip, I will make sure to devote more time to your training. In the meantime, you should sleep." He passed a hand over my forehead, and the scent of magic stung my nose as he spoke a Word.

My eyes grew heavy instantly, but the word 'trip' sent off an alarm bell, and I grabbed at his hand as he tried to pull away. "Don't go." Rylan's warning flashed in my head, and I realized that I'd never told Iannis about it.

"I have to go," Iannis sounded regretful, but firm. "I've already postponed my departure to deal with this, and I cannot do so any longer. My dirigible is already waiting, as are the rest of my delegates."

"You can't... go..." I tried to tell him, struggling against the sleep spell he put on me, but my tongue was thick, and my eyelids felt like anvils had been hung from my eyelashes. "It's... dangerous..."

"You'll be fine." I heard the smile in his voice. "So long as you stay here in the infirmary, in any case. The conference is only two weeks long, Sunaya. I'll be back soon enough."

His hand slipped from mine at the same time that the warning slipped from my mind, and I went under.

∾

WHEN I NEXT WOKE UP, it was to the sound of songbirds trilling outside my window. Opening my eyes, the first thing I saw was a table piled with an enormous amount of cards and flowers and candy. My stomach growled at the sight of a box of expensive hand-made chocolates, and it was then that I realized I felt well rested, much better than I had when I first woke.

But there was also a sense of unease in my gut, as though I'd left something unfinished, and I wasn't sure what it was.

"Guys, guys!" Noria squealed. "I think she's awake!"

I rolled over onto my back, and my eyes flew wide as I realized there were a whole bunch of people all seated around my bed. Noria, Comenius, Lakin, Elania, Annia, Elnos, Fenris – hell, even Director Chen was here, though she was standing by the foot of my bed rather than seated like the rest.

"By Magorah," I groaned, pushing myself up into a sitting position. "What is this, a wake or something? Did anyone make sure to embalm me first?"

"You're aliiiiive!" Noria squealed, throwing her arms around me. I grunted a little as she squeezed me tight.

"Yeah I'm alive, but not for long if you keep squeezing the air out of my lungs." Despite my words, I couldn't help the grin that spread over my face – her enthusiasm was infectious.

"We're so glad you're awake, Naya." Comenius was beaming. "When they told us what had happened to you we thought you wouldn't make it through the night."

"Yeah, I didn't think I was gonna make it either." I frowned, trying to remember the events of the past twenty-four hours, but the last thing I recalled was being stabbed in the neck by Danrian. "Damn it. Danrian got away, didn't he?"

"No, actually." Director Chen's cool voice drew my attention back to the foot of the bed. "Thanks to Enforcer Melcott and her task force, Warin Danrian was apprehended before he could get away."

"Really?" My eyes flew to Annia.

"Really." She grinned. "He's in a holding cell right now, awaiting another round of interrogation. He's resisting, but so far I've learned that the Shifter Royale was his own idea – there aren't any other Royales being run outside of Canalo."

"That's great." A weight I hadn't realized was on my chest eased up at the knowledge that we weren't going to have to shut down rings all across the Federation. Except... "Danrian told me that the Royale and the loans were all part of a bigger operation. Maybe he's the only one who was doing the Royales, but there's something else going on."

"I know. I'm digging into his background to see if there's anything I can use as leverage against him. Pretty sure I'll be able to get him to crack."

"Good." But I couldn't relax, not just yet. "What about Mika? And the other shifters? I'm guessing you guys must have gotten to me before Mika ripped my throat out, but were you able to save them all?"

"Yes," Lakin confirmed. "I went there with Fenris and several members of the Mages Guild, and between all of us we were able to contain Mika and return her and the other shifters to their senses. We also got one of the human staff members to lead us to the warehouse where they were keeping the rest."

"Which, by the way, included both Tylin and Nevin," Annia said. "So both of them made it back along with most of the others. You can thank their families for the huge pile of gifts by your bedside – they're all pretty grateful."

"That's great." I couldn't help but feel a twinge of sadness though. "I wish we could have gotten to them sooner."

Annia and I shared a look of understanding – we both knew that some of the families would never be getting their loved ones back.

"If it helps ease your mind, the Mages Guild has decided to

declare all the debts owed by shifters to Sandin Federal Bank null and void," Director Chen said gently. "Since the money was paid out with counterfeit gold it only seemed fair."

"Thank you." I smiled at Director Chen, feeling warmly toward her for the first time. "I'm sure the families will all be relieved."

"Yes," Director Chen said. "Congratulations on solving the case, Miss Baine. I'm sure your late mentor would be proud of you if he were here."

"Thanks, but it was really this guy you should be thanking." I turned toward Inspector Lakin. "If you hadn't started digging into Sillara's case, we never would have found out about any of this."

Lakin shook his head. "Maybe, but you and Annia did a lot of the heavy lifting, especially at the end. All those shifters are free because of you."

"I think we can all agree that Naya's the hero," Noria declared. "Hell, even your aunt is with me on this one. She sent you a thank you card for rescuing Mika."

My eyebrows shot up. "You're joking."

"No, she really did." Noria leaned back in her chair so she could grab one of the cards lying on my gift table. "Here, I'll find it for you."

"Director Chen! Director Chen!" Everyone turned toward the door as a grey-robed apprentice rushed into the infirmary. His cheeks were red from exertion, his long hair flying about, but it was the panic in his wide eyes that had me sitting up straight in alarm.

"What is it?" Director Chen asked, all business as she turned toward the apprentice. "It had better be very urgent for you to be barging in on us like this."

"It's about Lord Iannis!" the apprentice gasped. "The dirigible...!"

My veins turned to ice. "What?" I demanded, fisting my hands into the bedcovers. "What happened to the dirigible!"

The apprentice turned his wide-eyed gaze to me. "It never arrived at the capital. It's disappeared, and the entire delegation with it."

To be continued...

SUNAYA BAINE'S adventure continues in **Hunted by Magic**, Book 3 of the Baine Chronicles. Make sure to join her mailing list so you can be notified of future release dates, and to receive special updates, freebies and giveaways!

Join at www.jasminewalt.com/newsletter-signup

If you want to keep up with Jasmine Walt in the meantime, you can like her Facebook page, and follow her on Twitter, Goodreads, and Amazon.

DID YOU ENJOY THIS BOOK? Please consider leaving a review. Reviews help us authors sell books so we can afford to write more of them. Writing a review is the best way to ensure that the author writes the next one as it lets them know readers are enjoying their work and want more. Thank you very much for taking the time to read, and we hope you enjoyed the book!

GLOSSARY

Baine, Sunaya: a half-panther shifter, half-mage who hates mages and has a passion for justice. Because magic is forbidden to all but the mage families, Sunaya was forced to keep her abilities a secret until she accidentally used them to defend herself in front of witnesses. Rather than condemn her to death, the Chief Mage, Iannis ar'Sannin, chose to take her on as his apprentice, and now she struggles to balance her shifter and mage heritage.

Baine, Melantha: Sunaya's cousin, and daughter to the Jaguar Clan's Chieftain.

Baine, Mafiela: Chieftain of the Jaguar Clan and Sunaya's aunt.

Baine, Rylan: one of Chieftain Baine's least favored children, and Sunaya's cousin. He is an active member of the Resistance.

Benefactor, The: the name the Resistance call their anonymous, principal source of financial support. According to Sunaya's investigations, this mysterious criminal has many different irons in the fire.

Canalo: one of the fifty states making up the Northia Federation, located on the West Coast of the Northia Continent.

Chen, Lalia: the current Director of the Canalo Mages Guild in Solantha. She serves as deputy to Iannis ar'Sannin, the Chief Mage.

Chartis, Argon: former Director of the Canalo Mages Guild, dismissed by the Chief Mage for insubordination and attempts to undermine the Chief Mage's authority.

Chieftain: a title used to distinguish the head of a shifter clan.

Canter: an elderly mage often manning the reception at Solantha Palace.

Comenius Genhard: a hedgewitch from Pernia, owner of the shop Over the Hedge at Witches' End.

Creator, The: the ultimate deity, worshipped by all three races under different names.

Danrian, Warin: regional manager of the Sandin Federal Bank for Canalo.

Dara: capital of the Northia Federation, located on the east coast of the Northia Continent.

Enforcer: a bounty hunter employed by the government to seek out and capture wanted criminals. They operate under strict rules and are paid bounties for each head. While the majority of them are human, there is a strong minority of shifters, and even the occasional mage.

Enforcers' Guild: the administrative organization in charge of the Enforcers. Also, the building from which the various Enforcer crews work under their respective foremen.

Fenris: a clanless wolf shifter as well as good friend and confidant of Chief Mage Iannis ar'Sannin. No known last name.

Firegate Bridge: Solantha's best-known structure, a large red bridge spanning the length of Solantha Bay. It is accessible via Firegate Road.

Captain Galling: the human captain of the Enforcer's Guild in Solantha City, appointed by the former Chief Mage and Council.

Garai: the largest and most populated country on the Eastern Continent. Their people are known for their slanted eyes and ivory skin as well as their complicated, rune-like alphabet.

Garidano, Cirin: Finance Secretary of the State of Canalo.

Great Accord: a treaty struck by the ruling mages centuries ago which brought an end to a devastating war known as The Conflict. It is still the basis upon which mages rule their countries and territories. All new laws passed must be in accordance with the provisions of the Great Accord.

Herald, The: the main newspaper in Solantha City, geared towards the human majority population.

Iannis ar'Sannin: Chief Mage of Canalo. He resides in the capital city of Solantha, from which he runs Canalo as well as the Mages Guild with the help of his deputy. Originally a native of Manuc, a country located across the Eastern Sea.

Incidium: a powerful illegal drug that produces euphoria.

Kalois: a rare foreign plant which masks the smell of silver so well that shifters can be drugged or poisoned despite their sensitive noses.

Kan Zao: a mental and physical martial art tradition from Garai.

Lakin, Boon: a jaguar shifter from Parabas, recently appointed as Solantha's new Shiftertown Inspector following Roanas's death.

Loranian: the difficult, secret language of magic that all mages are required to master.

Mages Guild: the governmental organization that rules the mages in Canalo, and supervises the other races. The headquarters are in Solantha Palace. They are subordinate to the Chief Mage.

Main Crew: the largest group of Enforcers in the Guild.

They are generally favored over the other crews and get the most lucrative dockets.

Manuc: an island country off the west coast of the Central Continent.

Magorah: the god of the shifters, associated with the moon.

Maxon, Brin: Enforcer on the Main Crew. He is partnered with Nila Romana.

Melcott, Annia: a human Enforcer. She is a close friend of Sunaya's, and Noria's older sister.

Melcott, Noria: Annia Melcott's younger sister. A gifted inventor, she regularly tinkers with mechanical devices in between her college classes and her part-time job at Comenius's shop.

Northia Federation: a federation consisting of fifty states that cover the entire northern half and middle of the Western Continent. Canalo is part of this federation.

Over the Hedge: a shop at Witches' End selling magical charms and herbal remedies, belonging to Comenius Genhard.

Magi-tech: devices that are powered by both magic and technology.

Parabas: a city north of Solantha, outside the state of Canalo.

Pernia: a country on the Central Continent.

Prison Isle: an island in the middle of Solantha Bay that serves as a prison for Canalo's criminals.

Privacy Guard: a company leasing uniformed guards to governments and other institutions all over the Federation.

Ragga, Elnos: Noria Melcott's boyfriend. He is a student at Solantha academy and one of the few mages who believes in equality amongst the races. He and Noria can often be found working together, developing new magi-tech devices.

Resistance: a movement of revolutionaries and malcontents planning to overthrow the mages and take control of the Northia Federation.

Romana, Nila: a human Enforcer on the Main Crew and Brin Maxon's partner. She's known for relying on her looks first, her fighting skills second.

Rowanville: the only neighborhood of Solantha where all three races mix.

Sandin Federal Bank: a bank with branches in all fifty states of the Federation.

Shifter: a human who can change into animal form and back by magic; they originally resulted from illegal experiments by mages on ordinary humans.

Shifter Courier: a Solantha paper specifically geared towards the shifter population.

Shiftertown: the part of Solantha where the official shifter clans live.

Shiftertown Inspector: a shifter appointed by the Shiftertown Council to police shifter-related crime. He has deputies who assist him.

Solantha: the capital of Canalo State.

Solantha Palace: The seat of power in Canalo, where both the Chief Mage and the Mages Guild reside. It is located near the coast of Solantha Bay.

Talcon, Garius: the former Deputy Captain of the Enforcer's Guild. Sunaya discovered he was in league with Petros Yantz, the man behind the silver murders, and killed him in self-defense.

Tanzarite: a rare semi-precious stone.

Tarenan, Sillara: a shifter Enforcer and early victim of the silver murders.

Tillmore, Roanas: The former Shiftertown Inspector and father figure/mentor to Sunaya. He was poisoned while digging into the silver murders, prompting Sunaya to take over the investigation.

Traxtoline: an explosive material, expensive and unstable.

The Twilight: a bar in Rowanville where Sunaya used to bartend.

Ur-God: the name the humans call the Creator by.

Vance: Foreman of the Enforcer's Guild's Main Crew.

Witches' End: a pier in Solantha City, part of the Port, where immigrant magic users sell their wares and services.

Yantz, Petros: the former Chief Editor of the Herald. He fled the city after Sunaya discovered he was behind the silver murders, and is still at large.

ACKNOWLEDGMENTS

Thank you very much to the awesome volunteers who helped beta read and proofread this book. Your spot-on feedback and eagle eyes have saved my butt more times than I can count.

Thank you also to Mary Burnett, my writing partner and editor. Working with you has been great fun so far, and we've accomplished more than I could have imagined in such a short time.

And of course, thank you to my illustrator and the love of my life, Judah Dobin. You're my biggest supporter in everything and I am ridiculously lucky to have you.

ABOUT THE AUTHOR

New York Times and USA Today Bestselling Author Jasmine Walt is a devourer of books, chocolate, and all things martial arts. Somehow, those three things melded together in her head and transformed into a desire to write, usually fantastical stuff with a healthy dose of action and romance. Her characters are a little (okay, a lot) on the snarky side, and they swear, but they mean well. Even the villains sometimes.

When Jasmine isn't chained to her keyboard, you can find her working on her dao sword form, spending time with her family, or binge-watching superhero shows on Netflix.

Want to connect with Jasmine? You can find her on Instagram at @jasmine.walt, on Facebook, or at www.jasminewalt.com.

ALSO BY JASMINE WALT

The Baine Chronicles Series:

Burned by Magic

Bound by Magic

Hunted by Magic

Marked by Magic

Betrayed by Magic

Deceived by Magic

Scorched by Magic

Tested by Magic (Novella)

Forsaken by Magic (Novella)

The Nia Rivers Adventures

Dragon Bones

Demeter's Tablet

Templar Scrolls

Serpent Mound

Eden's Garden

The Gatekeeper Chronicles

Marked by Sin

Hunted by Sin

Claimed by Sin

The Dragon's Gift Trilogy

Printed in Great Britain
by Amazon